SINFUL SAINT

SINNERS & SAINTS
BOOK 1

LANA SKY

Sinful Saint

Sinful Saint By Lana Sky

Cover Design and Interior Formatting by Charity Chimni
Editing by Charity Chimni
Alpha Reading by Jessica Rita Rampersad

Originally published as Sinners & Saints.

ACKNOWLEDGMENTS

Thanks so much to everyone who supported this draft along the way, including the many beta readers who provided encouragement! Please keep in mind that this story includes dark, graphic, and explicit content matter that may not be suitable for readers under the age of 18—or for readers who are uncomfortable with the following subject matter: drug use, mentions of suicide, cultish behavior, explicit sex, and graphic depictions of violence.

ONE

MY BROTHER KILLED himself because of me. He never said as much out loud, but there's only so many times you can pick at someone before they shatter. Before love sours into resentment. Before they hate so much, it kills them—and Hale hated me, right up until the end.

I deserved it.

That's what kills most about his suicide. I nagged him. I shunned him. I turned my back as our father ostracized him. And there's really only one way to atone for the sins I've committed.

I deserve to die, just as he did.

In the days leading up to this moment, I convinced myself it would be easy. I would leave early under the pretense of working the morning shift at the soup kitchen. Instead, I'd take the longer path through the outskirts of the city, where Springer Bridge serves as the entrance to one of the municipal parks. The area is all but deserted this time of day.

There's no one to watch me climb over this metal rail and let go.

A simple theory on paper but far harder to put into practice. I didn't account for the guilt or the anxiety weighing on my chest to the point it hurts to breathe. I startle at every sound to break the quiet, and I'm just praying the sun doesn't fully rise before I gather up the nerve to...

Do it. Jump. Can I even climb over the rail? My legs are shaking, and I keep fiddling with the golden cross around my neck. It was my grandmother's. *Suicide is a sin,* she used to say. *Jesus died for you, and to sin is to forsake that gift.*

At least she isn't alive to see me now. Jesus wasted his gift on me. My sins can't be paid for, not after what I've done.

Nothing drills that in more than the cell phone persistently buzzing against my palm. Each incoming message is a glaring reminder of the few options I have left.

We're meant to be, Colton wrote, the first in a series of texts. *It's never too late to be saved, Frances. I forgive you.*

Of course, he does. Every member of Covenant wholly believes salvation lurks within the walls of the church. Forgiveness should come as easily as breathing. *Unless* you're my mother, or Hale, or anyone else bold enough to step a toe out of line.

Then you're damned to Hell. Like me too, I guess. At least I won't be alone.

With a sigh, I tear my gaze from the screen and look down. Instantly, a little more of my bravery peels away. I'm so high up. The hem of my sweater ripples in the wind, disrupting my view of the water below. Ironically, it's one of the last things Hale ever bought me. Before the anger. The hate. The lies.

God, the fabric still smells like him. I inhale deeply, chasing traces of him amongst the stench of the bay. My eyes burn, but blinking doesn't stop the tears. They stream endlessly as my cell phone screen ignites with another message.

Where are you? It's Father. *Colton says you haven't checked in yet.*

More guilt seeps in, going to war with my fragile resolve. Rather than reply, I shove the device into my pocket. Then I push everyone from my brain but *him*. I try to recall his face or his voice... I'd give anything to see him again.

Anything.

It seems God, however, has chosen a crueler punishment for me than death—endless grief. Despite how hard I cling to this cross, Hale is still gone. After a million prayers, the pain slicing through my heart hasn't eased. Desperate, I close my eyes and reach out with my other hand...

That was another thing Granny told me—*If you trust your faith, you can accomplish anything, Frances.*

As my fingers tremble in the frigid air, grasping nothing, I can't escape the dark thoughts haunting me since the day Hale died. *You love him so much, huh? But you barely remember him as he was before...*

It's true. Three months, and almost every trace of my older brother, is a blurred smear on my psyche *but* that night. The one when I found his body slumped against an embroidered chaise, a needle in his arm and a lit cigarette in a crystal ashtray resting by his side. Even now, I close my eyes and still see him—a pale body so gaunt and lifeless it could have been a stranger's. Not handsome, cocky Hale with eyes so blue they rivaled the sky.

All that remains of him are the two things he left for me to find, both of which are in my pocket. I open my eyes and withdraw them—the first is a crumpled flyer for Covenant's Salvation program, Father's crowning glory. In essence, it's a charity. Through it, he's been able to use his ample resources to help many of the city's poor, and most in the church, myself included, have volunteered there.

Only, in the final weeks of his life, Hale called it a scam. At the time, I thought he was being too cynical. Through Salvation, the homeless were provided with three hot meals daily, and the disenfranchised were assisted with finding employment. Father could be overbearing, but he only wanted to uphold the tenants of our faith. In the end, though, Hale turned his back on that too. I still don't know why he hated us so much. Our father. Or me.

Beside this flyer, he left an equally-battered empty pack of cigarettes with a doodle etched on the back in ink. My heart pangs as I trace the jagged lines that make up the visage of a skull with angel wings. It's morbid but stunning in its detail—a sign of how far from the righteous path he'd strayed, yet he didn't seem ashamed of his fall from grace. Maybe he needed to break away from Father's control in the end. Unlike me, he had real talent, destined for more than volunteer work.

I think that's why he left these two things behind. To tell me in the only way he knew how, *This is what you drove me to, Frey. This is what I became because of you. A monster.* Our father's strict, perfect world never fit him, and the only outlet he had was through cigarettes, booze, and drugs.

And death.

I choke back the memory—but nothing erases the image of him, his eyes empty and staring.

Not scripture.

Not prayer.

Not guilt.

Nothing.

A roar of thunder echoes in the distance as if to punctuate that hopeless reality. I'll never find peace, and in stinging lashes, rain comes down, slicking the railing and making it harder to grasp. I lean forward to stay centered, feeling the moisture soak through the front of my navy skirt.

As gray daylight tinges the horizon, I know it won't be long before traffic picks up, and I risk being spotted. Panic gnaws away at my few remaining shreds of determination. *What are you doing, Frey?*

What am I doing?

Spiraling. Standing on a bridge, separated from the edge by only a thin rail. And for what? There are other ways to make

Father suffer. Other ways to avenge Hale. Other ways to punish myself.

But this is the only option I'm capable of. Inhaling raggedly, I tighten my grip on the rail, prepared to climb over it...

The wind must pick up, tousling my hair amid a burst of heat. Heat that smells like smoke and musk. My spine tingles as if I'm being watched. *Wait.* I don't even get the chance to turn around before my fear is confirmed.

"You gonna do it already, or what?"

The voice—deep and masculine—drips into my ear and startles me so badly that I slip. My heart drops through my body, and I swear I see it fall into the water down below. Luckily, my grip keeps me upright, and I pant, desperate to regain my bearings.

As I do, the terror I've fought to keep at bay breaks loose—*I can't do this.* My fingers tremble, slick with rainwater, and I loosen my grip. *I can't do this!*

"Hey!" Two fingers speckled with grime snap beneath my nose. "Look at me."

Shivering, I turn to finally take in the imposing stranger at my back.

He's tall. Too tall. Wild blond hair drapes his shoulders, longer than mine. He's kept it loosely tied in a ponytail, but the wind already ripped most of it free. Stray strands fall across his face, obscuring a pair of bloodshot gray eyes.

Alarm shoots down my spine as they connect with mine. I've never seen someone sport such an expression, teeth bared, brows drawn.

"Did you hear me?" he demands. The deep tone of his voice rivals another roll of thunder.

Years of obedience betray me. I can't stop myself from croaking out, "W-What?"

I haven't pleased him. Those gray eyes narrow further. "You gonna jump or what?" He jerks his chin toward the rough water down below. The motion conveys a universal expression—*I'm waiting.* "Some of us need to use this space too, Princess."

Use? I stare, too stunned to reply. I shouldn't be. I spent hours rehearsing what I'd say if someone found me. Never did I imagine them berating me for not being fast enough.

"You think you can hurry the fuck up?" He scoffs, rolling his eyes as my cheeks flame at the vulgarity. "You aren't the only one who needs some peace with the deep blue, so get on with it already."

Peace? The way he hissed that word sticks out to me. He has a smoker's voice. Gritty and grated—a fitting match for his smell—sweat and alcohol. A lot of it. That must be why his eyes are so red.

Like Hale, he's crammed his veins full of vice and sin.

I should be repulsed by him, but I can't take my eyes off him.

"Hey!" He slashes his hand through the air. "You ain't the only one with problems, sweetheart."

Irritation breaks through the fear, and I consider leaving. But being a coward was what drove Hale from me in the first place. I couldn't defend him to our father, and I can't even defend my right to follow him. *Get a backbone, Frey.*

Channeling my anger, I try. "Leave me alone—"

"It's not that hard, sweetheart." The stranger grabs my shoulder, and I'm paralyzed. "Either jump... or move."

"S-Stop!" I try to buck him off, but he grips my forearm instead. I should be screaming. Only God knows why I'm not. It could be his lack of pressure. Or his voice, relentlessly authoritative.

I've spent my entire life obeying men who speak with a fraction of the conviction he does.

"Move," he commands.

The Frey from a few days ago would listen. Not anymore. *Grow a backbone,* Hale told me. So, I crane my head back and perform the first action that comes to mind.

I spit, right in his face.

Shock travels through his entire body, and my gaze is drawn like a magnet down the length of him, tracking the reaction. His shoulders tense beneath a gray sweatshirt speckled with stains. Dark stains.

Fresh. My nostrils flare, catching the stench of copper...

As he swipes at his mouth, the substance on his hands is easier to make out—a bright, glistening red. Not dirt.

Blood?

Judging from the lack of open wounds on his knuckles, it isn't his.

I FEEL DIZZY. The world dangerously begins to tilt, and I tighten my grip over the rail, fighting to stay upright. I've never seen blood like that.

Not so much of it.

"Hey." Aware of where my gaze is, he tucks the hand behind him. Then he advances, grabbing my arm again. Guttural, his voice overpowers the scream I choke out. "You wanna jump? Why?"

I blink. A threat should have come next, not a deceptively simple question.

"Why?" I counter breathlessly.

"That's what I said." He spits on the pavement and makes a "get on with it" motion with his finger. Grime caked under the nail draws my eye. It matches the muck slathered all over his jeans and scuffed-up black boots.

More blood?

Or perhaps just dirt. He's filthy.

"Come on, and fucking say it," he goads. "Impress me, sweetheart."

I bristle at his tone. He's serious.

"Get the *fuck* away from me," I hiss, copying his coarse language. My cheeks sear as if to betray me. I'm not this person, and years of etiquette kick in, making me tack on, "Please—"

"And why should I do that?" He puffs up, impossibly large. A bear of a figure goading me on. It's like he's feeding off the anger. Mine especially.

All I can do to counter him is ask, "Why does it even matter to you?"

"I'm curious. What's your bullshit reason?" he demands. "Boyfriend dump your ass? The kiddies on the playground being mean to you?"

I flinch. If only those stupid problems were all I had to contend with.

"My brother killed himself because of me," I croak. "How is that for a reason?"

It's the first time I've said those words out loud, and they sting like hell. For months, we've pretended that Hale had an accident. An illness. A heart attack at twenty-six.

Even his obituary omitted the truth. I wanted to believe Father did so out of concern for *Hale*'s legacy—not his own. Looking back, I hate myself for trying to rationalize it. Of course, his motives were selfish. He didn't want the stigma to ruin his image as the perfect political candidate with the perfect family.

Or he couldn't face the guilt.

"That it?" the stranger demands.

Confused, I look up to find him raising an eyebrow. It's overgrown, stretching across his forehead, almost meeting the other one.

I wish it made him unattractive. More like a scary monster meant to be feared. Or a demon, perhaps? Hell sent him to me as punishment for my sins. A malicious smile would help enforce that characterization, but he's frowning instead, his gaze distant. If anything, his rugged visage resembles a fallen angel who didn't feel like going south. He decided to roam Westpoint City instead.

And torment me.

Father warned me about the danger of strangers—and this man more than fits the bill. He looks dirty. Dangerous. Tattooed. I make out a hint of black ink forming a design that stretches beneath the collar of his sweatshirt and swallow hard. It's probably gang-related.

There are so many clues warning me to run that it's unthinkable that I haven't.

"No wonder you wanna jump," he adds, drawing my attention back to his face. "With that shitty-ass reason. Well, go on then. Be my guest."

My throat tightens as I sag against the railing. It's one thing to have someone try and stop me. Another entirely to have that same person give me permission.

Apparently, he thinks I'm pathetic, too.

"Well? I'm waiting." He wipes his mouth again, unconcerned by the blood coating his hand. To erase my spit, I realize, horrified. Anger isn't what I find in his stare, though. Just apathy. "You might as well jump already."

"Fine." It's childish to counter him, but I can't resist the irritation he inspires in me. It's sharp and prickling, goading me to act out of character. Rebel.

I've been numb for so long that the anger itches.

Gritting my teeth, I turn back to the railing, but I don't make it far in my quest to jump.

"Wait—" one of his hands finds mine before I can move, pinning it flat against the barrier. His warmth is a shock. Only Colton touches me these days—his father all but paid for the right after all, with his generous donations to my father. That doesn't make him a bad person, though. Money is the weapon Father uses to further his holy cause, and Colton is a good man from a prominent family. Everyone says so, along with rampantly speculating that an engagement is on the horizon. The strange part? I barely know him. I'm not even sure what his favorite color is. This man, however?

I get the sense he likes red. Red like the blood on his hands.

"S-Stop!" I resist the contact but don't let go of the rail. Below, the dizzying scope of the view sucks me in. I only need to lean forward and let gravity do the rest. "Let go of me!"

"No."

Suddenly, his fingers clamp down and yank mine loose from the railing. I stagger back, grasping instinctively for a stable surface. The only thing within reach is something I clench unseen. Something round. Warm. Hard as stone.

"Fuck." With a grunt, the guy jerks his forearm from my grip before I even register grabbing him. I must have gripped too hard because he rubs at the spot, hissing through his teeth. In the blink of an eye, he recovers, positioning himself at the railing where I once stood.

I plant my feet, panting and dazed. "What are you doing?"

"Enforcing the rules," he snarls. "For that stupid ass answer, you've lost your right to jump here."

"Who...who do you think you are?"

He throws his head back to propel a glob of spit over the rail. "Someone with more goddamn problems than you."

"I'll just go somewhere else," I stammer.

"No." His voice rings with that unnerving authority. "You're going to tell me more. Your brother offed himself. Why?"

I wince. In his gruff baritone, it sounds so much worse. Final. "What kind of question is that?"

"A simple one." He shrugs, completely unbothered by my reaction. "Can you answer it or not?"

Shock wipes my mind blank. Once again, he's asked something no one else has.

"Why... Why does it even matter?"

"It matters to you." He cuts his eyes in my direction, but the intensity in them shouldn't be there. No one has ever looked at me like this. Not Father. Not even Hale. Certainly not Colton. He tells me to pray the pain away. This man seems to think differently. He wants me to verbalize it.

It matters.

"Why do you think he did it?" he adds.

My lips part to issue a rehearsed answer. *Because he was troubled.* That's what Father would want me to say.

"Because our father didn't accept him," I croak instead. My voice comes out halting. It feels strange to be so honest—as dangerous as standing on the ledge of a bridge. "He hated trying to please him. He hated *us.* I... I still don't know why."

It sounds paranoid, but I know deep down that it's exactly how Hale always felt.

Like an outsider.

"You really think it's *his* fault then. Your father's. That's what I'm hearing. So, you decide to off yourself, to punish him?" The stranger laughs. "Word of advice, there are a million other ways to punish your old man than jumping off a damn bridge. Go find some tattooed little punk to screw. That should piss him off."

He keeps laughing. Apparently, he finds that concept amusing.

"Like *you*?" I want it to be an insult, but my eyes are on his neck. From this angle, I have a clearer view of the design snaking across his collarbone. Something intricate, made of swirls of ink. A skull?

He turns his head before I can be sure, and my breath catches. His gaze is like ice. Hard. Impenetrable. The longer I meet his stare, the more unsteady I feel. When he finally looks away, butterflies flutter to life in my stomach, swarming with foreboding.

I get the sense that everything about me was summed up in that one look. His ultimate determination?

"Not interested," he tells me coldly. "Now run along. You don't belong here."

"You can't...you can't do this." The moment the words leave my mouth, I realize what I'm doing—whining about a spot to die in. There are other places along this bridge to jump and no one else to stop me.

I swivel toward a random direction and take a step.

"Wait." He cocks his head as if listening for something. I hear it, too, a noise that sends my pulse racing—the swell of police sirens coming from across the bridge. *Oh no.* A million different explanations come to mind. Father could have called them. Or this man could be an escaped convict. I toy with both ideas, but neither one inspires the alarm it should.

Just impatience. The thought of returning home weighs on my mind, more terrifying than the prospect of jumping off a bridge. It's selfish, I know—but I can't go back to pretending that nothing is wrong. I can't. Apparently, I'm not the only one eager to avoid discovery.

"Fuck," the stranger hisses. "We need to move." He whirls around but surprises me by snatching my wrist.

"We?" I gasp. "Let go of me!"

"I can't focus with all this goddamn noise," he snarls in return. "Unless you want to stick around for the cops. No? Then come on."

He storms toward the path, pulling me behind him. Despite digging my heels into the pavement, I can't find enough leverage to resist him. He's so strong.

Helpless, I try to raise my voice, scanning the bridge for anyone in view. "What are you doing?"

His laughter echoes ominously, reinforcing just how alone we truly are. There isn't even a car on the road.

"You scared?" He cranes his neck to see my expression and scoffs. "I guess you're not that eager to die, are you, sweetheart?"

My thoughts stall. Restart. As seems to be the norm where he is concerned, vulgarity is the only weapon I can utilize right away. This time, I use a curse favored by Hale. "Fuck you—"

"Already told you that you're not my type." Undeterred, he keeps moving, easily dragging me toward the park's main entrance.

My heart races as I consider where he could be taking me. Nowhere good. Suicide I'd planned for. Not... Murder.

Though this would certainly be an easier route to my original end goal.

With a hard tug, my captor pulls me closer. "Come on."

"Let go!" My teeth chatter. The breeze is merciless this close to the shore. A tiny hint of regret sneaks in before I can quash it down. If only I knew my suicide would be foiled. I might have worn my sneakers instead of a pair of sandals.

The further we move from the bridge, however, the warmer it feels. It's been so long since I've been in this part of the city alone—outside of a limo or a volunteer group. Here the air feels different. Grittier.

The sounds are louder, and when we leave the quiet confines of the park, the bustling heart of downtown intrudes with all the subtlety of a brick wall.

It's all noise. All chaos—masses of impatient people rushing off to their destinations. None seem to notice or care about the young woman pulled relentlessly by a stranger.

"You got any money on you?" he demands while simultaneously hauling me across an intersection.

Up ahead, a bus trudges around a corner, and I stop in my tracks. An advertisement takes up the entire length of the vehicle—one sporting a picture of smiling, beautiful people bathed in golden sunlight. In the center stands a handsome man with graying blond hair and a warm smile.

Learn the Beauty of Hope, reads the slogan printed underneath him. *Become one of the collective.*

I stare until the bus lurches around a corner. It's a promo photo from a years' old campaign, one of the few to survive the recent purge considering Father supposedly stepped aside as Shepherd during his election campaign. Publicly anyway.

"Hey, Blondie!"

I startle to awareness on the edge of a curb and throw my hand out to get my bearings. Automatically, my fingers capture something warm. Pulsing. Alive. A man's arm, I see, looking up. *His*. Visibly annoyed, he fixes me with a probing stare, and I tense in anticipation of what he might say next.

"Do you got any money?"

"What?"

He scoffs. "I'll take that as a no."

He continues down the block, using my arm as a leash. I can't resist risking a glance over my shoulder, hunting for a police car or one of the black vans belonging to Covenant. All I find is the typical mid-morning traffic, and some of the fear building in my stomach eases.

Though, Father should be the least of my worries. I inspect the filthy hand latched onto my wrist and consider the fact that, for all intents and purposes, I'm being kidnapped—not that my kidnapper seems particularly concerned with stealth.

I could always scream. Cause a scene. Wouldn't that make for an interesting headline? *Frances Heywood, Rescued Mid-Kidnapping.*

Another potential headline comes to mind next, one far more morbid. *Frances Heywood—Missing, Never Found.*

"Hey!" I jump as the stranger snaps his fingers again, directly under my nose. "I said, what do you want? And keep in mind that you owe me for this."

This being whatever he plans to get from a roadside coffee truck we're standing in front of. I didn't even notice we stopped. The whole structure is battered, painted in camo, and a mural displays a stylized version of a Harley motorcycle and the words "Motorway Coffee" in block lettering.

"Let me do the talking," the stranger warns as he approaches the counter. His posture is relaxed, his tone cordial. "I'll take two regulars. Just add it to my tab, Ben. You know I'm good for it."

The man, Ben, nods. "You got it, D. When the hell did you get back in town? I thought you were cutting out for good..."

He trails off, his eyes on my face. My cheeks flame, and I'm suddenly self-conscious. Does he recognize me? With Father's campaign in full swing, who knows.

Though it's been weeks since I've shown up for his speeches or political events to play the role of dutiful daughter—not for lack of trying on Colton's part. *A dutiful woman honors her father above all,* he likes to say.

"Ah... Let's say I changed my mind." The stranger laughs, raking a hand through the tangle of hair that fell out of its ponytail.

"Well, you look like shit," Ben declares, crossing his arms. He's tall in such a small space, towering against the ceiling of the truck. His battered leather jacket hangs open, revealing the black shirt beneath and ample muscle straining the cotton. "I hope your presence here doesn't mean you've stuck your nose into more trouble."

Long dark hair enhances his piercing brown eyes that again fixate in my direction. "Who's your friend?"

The man beside me releases my arm and shrugs. "No one. You ready with those coffees?"

"In a minute."

While pouring two cups of coffee, Ben turns his attention to my companion. His jaw is clenched, enhancing the intimidation cast by his appearance as a whole. While not as dirty, he's every bit as disarming as the blond man. His neck even sports a similar tattoo, obscured by the collar of his T-shirt and leather jacket. "If you plan to stick around, I hope it's for good this time. To reconnect. With the boys—"

"Me, play well with others?" The stranger flashes a grin that makes me suck in a breath. "I don't think so."

"Oh really?" Ben sets the coffee pot aside and leans over the counter. "I think you should reconsider. Maybe your new *friend*—" He cuts his gaze to me, this time homing in on my face. "Will make you realize what I've been trying to tell you from the goddamn start. We *need* you. That crazy fucker's going to get us all killed—"

"Just the coffee today, Ben," the stranger says over him. He flashes another grin, but the expression doesn't reach his eyes. "No jokes, just the joe. Please."

"Whatever you say, D. Here—" Ben slams two steaming cups on the counter.

"About damn time." The stranger, D, shoves one cup at me. Then he places his hand on my lower back and hastens me along the street.

"What was that about?" I ask. Paranoia has me glancing back, but Ben has already turned his attention to another customer. Still, I swear I see him cock his head to shoot one last searching look our way.

"Nothing." D picks up his pace, urging me along. "Keep moving."

I shudder at the feel of his massive palm. Desperate for a distraction, I stare at the black lid of my cup, one eyebrow raised. "Is this your idea of talking me out of—" I swallow down the word "jumping" and sigh instead. "Coffee?"

Rather than answer, he blows into the lid of his drink and takes a sip, grimacing at the taste. "That's some good shit." Head cocked, he eyes the sky. "I want to show you something. Come on."

He moves past me, cutting through a group of yawning students, their backpacks dangling from their shoulders. A few paces away, he glances back. "You coming, or what?"

Or what? a part of me whispers. I should take my chance and make a break for the bridge. I should focus on the only plan that's made sense since losing Hale. I should go.

"Suit yourself." With a grunt, my reluctant savior takes another sip of coffee and continues his slow, steady stroll onward.

I definitely shouldn't follow. I start to turn away, but from the corner of my eye, I catch sight of a dark car maneuvering through traffic a block down. My heart hammers so badly I nearly drop the coffee.

It's suspiciously sleek, far more expensive than the vehicles surrounding it. One of Father's?

Kidnapping me wouldn't be the worst thing he's done, but it's my potential destination that makes me shield my face with my free hand. He threatened it once, should I spurn his wishes. *"You need prayer, Frey. Time to grieve. Perhaps the compound is the only way for you to regain your peace..."*

The same place had supposedly "saved" Hale. Look what happened to him.

The stranger is nearly to the end of the block when I finally stagger a few steps forward.

"Don't forget the coffee," he shouts back without turning around.

I look at the road for any sign of the car, but it's gone.

And yet I don't feel any safer.

THREE

I HAVEN'T WALKED around by myself in so long. Not by choice. Technically, I'm not allowed to. The members of Father's congregation call him The Shepherd, and I think he took that title to heart. For six years, he's treated me like a lamb, one too stupid to fend for itself.

Or marked for sacrifice, forever soiled if it strays too far from the herd.

A part of me knows it wasn't all his fault—when Covenant caught on in popularity, the attention came with positive and negative facets. Such as death threats. Whenever Father wasn't watching my every move, his most trusted associate, Robbie, would. At least until recently. Hale's death and an unexpectedly bitter political campaign ironically worked to my benefit. Both drew his attention from me for the time being, though I know which one affects him more. No one expected the newcomer candidate focused on religion and crime reduction to come so close to unseating a popular incumbent. Only single digits separate them in most polls, and the mere specter of a victory has made Father fixate even more on appearances and image.

It must be going on an hour, maybe two, since I was supposed to arrive at Salvation. I wonder if he's waiting there for me, Colton in tow. His texts alluded to that very scenario, though I don't have the heart to pull out my phone and check if he's sent any more.

"You coming?" the stranger asks from up ahead. "I ain't waiting for ya, Blondie."

And yet, he's remained within my view this entire time. Increasing my pace, I catch up just as the next light turns red.

"This way." He shoulders his way through the crowd, sipping his coffee all the while.

Warily, I copy him, surprised by the taste. It's good, and I find myself inhaling it, sloshing scalding liquid down my chin with every step.

The pain barely cuts through the numb chill haunting me since the funeral. All I feel is a faint, pulsing buzz in my skin as we enter a quieter, more run-down area of the city I'm not familiar with.

I'm a princess far from her gilded cage. Grass and weeds poke up through cracks in the sidewalk as buildings become smaller, some speckled with graffiti and sporting windows nailed shut with plywood. Ironically, this is the type of place a Salvation group might volunteer.

Or advise as too dangerous to venture in alone.

With every step we take, the man beside me tenses up. Soon, his shoulders are a firm line, his head lowered.

"What's wrong?" I glance around but find no obvious threats nearby.

"This way," he snaps, abruptly changing direction. "Hurry up...and keep your head down, for fuck's sake."

I watch him cut through a narrow alley, and my heart skips a beat before I follow him in. Halfway through, he shoulders open a battered door and jerks his chin toward the shadowed interior. "Stay close to me."

Unease flutters down my spine, keeping me in place as one pressing question bounces off the inside of my skull—*What are you doing?*

I glance down at my bare toes and can't come up with an answer.

"You coming, or what?" the stranger demands. A hint of impatience seeps into his voice, and I look up to find his eyes narrowed—but fixed somewhere over my shoulder. I copy him but discover only an overflowing trash can.

Regardless, he's on edge. His unease itches at my nerves, making me fidget with the lid of my coffee cup. Maybe I'm not the only one expecting to be followed?

But if Father's security detail is on my tail, they seem content to observe for now.

"Earth to Blondie."

He's talking to me, utilizing a nickname that makes my belly flip. Am I insulted? I'm not sure. His voice is softer than it should be, I think. As if it's more than a harmless moniker, but a name meant only for me.

"Come on." He barrels through the doorway impatiently.

Shaking my head to clear it, I force myself to take another step. Then another until I approach the entrance. He lurks just inside, holding the door open. His bulk alone nearly takes up the entirety of a small hallway. It's dark beyond him. A strange smell lingers in the air that I can't name. Something salty. Musky. Sweat?

I head toward it absently and nearly trip.

"Watch your step."

In vain of his warning, my foot hits the edge of a ledge descending to a lower level. As soon as I sway, he's by my side, placing a steadying hand on my hip to keep me upright. With his guidance, I stagger down a few more steps before the floor evens out. There, he retreats, and my only souvenir of his touch is a persistent, prickling heat that doesn't fade.

"Where are we?" I blink until I can make out a large room beyond him. Square. Orange walls. Concrete floors.

Artificial lights illuminate the space where a black mat dominates the center. Scattered weights and exercise equipment have been stacked in the corners. A flicker of movement draws my attention to my left, just in time to witness him stripping his sweatshirt.

Suddenly, my coffee cup slides against sweat-soaked fingers. I barely tighten my grip in time, and my reward is a lukewarm splash of liquid over my wrist, along with plenty of shame to heat my cheeks.

"See something you like?" He holds my gaze while tossing the gray hoodie aside. "It's rude to stare at a man like he's a piece of meat."

"No," I choke out, barely able to maintain eye contact.

Some might objectify him as a piece of toned, very *ripped* meat—and that's an understatement. What had been disguised as shapeless bulk before is pure, solid muscle, streaked with silvery scars and ebony tattoos.

He's beautiful in a broken way. Like Hale's battered cigarette pack drawing. The jagged lines paint his skin, nearly every inch of it. One design in particular spans his entire back—a giant relief of a skeleton riding a black horse with a mane curling around his ribcage. They taught us a story in Bible study once—the four horsemen of the apocalypse. I guess he took that tale literally.

"You gonna stare or make yourself useful?" He gestures toward a corner of the room, and his rippling muscles distort the horseman, robbing some of the intensity from the design. "Come on. I need to spar."

I sputter like an idiot. "S-spar?"

"Chop chop!" He points to the corner again, and I notice an object lying there. It's square and made of the same material as the center mat, almost like a pillow. "Hold it up," he barks.

I set my coffee down to comply, and he dishes out another order.

"Get onto the mat."

Trapped in the narrow space, I swallow as he advances. While I wasn't looking, he grabbed a roll of gauze. As he moves, he wraps a length of it around both fists, forming a makeshift glove over the bloodied surfaces. Then he claps harshly to command my attention. "Square your stance."

He scoffs when I don't move.

"I... I don't know what that means," I blurt out.

He rolls his eyes. "For fuck's sake. Spread your legs."

He advances, and I jump, wrestling with the choice to stay or run. Too late. He's already nudging one of my feet with the toe of his foot. His nearness this time hits differently with his chest bare.

I've never been this close to a shirtless man. Not even Colton. Sometimes he pushed me to go further than kissing. Once, his fingers grazed my inner thigh before I managed to talk him out of it.

We both knew our boundaries.

This reaction, however, is violent. This man doesn't smell like Colton—the scent flooding my nostrils is sharper than mild cologne. Harsher. My thoughts swim with every inhale. I'm dizzy.

Until he grabs my wrist. Fire shoots down the length of my

arm, and I gasp at the sensation—but he doesn't give me the chance to interpret it fully.

"Arms up. No, not like that!" Sighing, he steps in closer.

Close enough that I get a sharp whiff of salt and something more pungent. Maybe aftershave. Maybe blood. It cloys in my lungs as he braces both hands over my shoulders and yanks them into alignment.

"You hurt someone," I blurt out in a rush. By the time I gather the nerve to meet his gaze, he's staring at the wall behind me. "Didn't you?"

"Chin up," he barks before returning to his attacking pose. "Now raise the pad. Yeah, like that. Now brace." Lightning-quick, he lashes out, striking the center of the pad with a clenched fist.

The blow rocks me back on my heels, and I stagger to stay upright.

"Good." Flexing his shoulder, he lands another strike over the mat.

Another. Each hit rattles me to my core, and I dig my toes into the floor to find enough leverage to keep standing. Not that he seems to care. His focus is turned inward as his breaths quicken and deepen. This is calming to him.

Movement and violence.

Talking about it, on the other hand, doesn't seem to be on his mind.

"Who... Who are you?" I choke out in between hits.

"Chin up."

He lashes out before I can react, cupping my jaw himself. His warmth is such a contrast to the chill in the room. I flinch, and in response, his fingertips press tighter, forcing me to meet his gaze.

And *those eyes*. They blaze, boring directly into mine.

"Nothing else matters but anticipating my movements," he insists through gritted teeth. "Remember that. Now block!"

"Wait!" I barely manage to get the pad up in time. The blow still knocks the wind out of me, and I hunch over, gasping for air.

"Is this...how...you treat everyone?" I wonder in between pants. "By beating them senseless minutes after first meeting?"

He laughs, but the sound resembles a sigh more than anything. "Sweetheart, did anyone ever tell you that you don't know how to shut the fuck up?"

My face heats. Ironically, no one has ever told me I talk too much. If anything, it's been the opposite. Hale, for one, hated that I was too silent. Too meek. Too afraid. I never defended him.

"No," I admit softly. "What about you?"

"Easy, tiger." He laughs again while pivoting to the left. "We're not here to talk. Rather than bore me to death, show me what you've got. I'm sure you must have some anger stored somewhere in that body of yours. Let's go—" he snatches the mat and holds it up before his chest. Then, with a come-hither wave, he beckons me closer. "Hit me!"

The movement exposes his chest to me completely, and my throat goes dry. My view distorts until his tattoo is all I see.

A skull with angel wings.

Just like the one Hale drew.

FOUR

HE SNAPS his fingers as I freeze. "Hey! Earth to Blondie."

From this angle, the tattoo glistens beneath a sheen of sweat, and I have no idea how I missed it before.

It's grotesquely beautiful. Black ink forms the base—a vivid contrast to the hue of the skull's eyes. Unlike his other designs, both orbs have been etched in ruby-red ink. Blood-red. Extending from the skeletal visage are two stylized wings. Angel wings.

"That—" I point to it with a trembling finger, but that isn't enough. I stumble toward him and run my thumb along the angel wings, feeling the contours for myself. It doesn't vanish, pulsing and alive.

"Hey!" He flinches out of my reach as I wrench the cigarette pack from my pocket.

"Look!" Viewing it now beside his tattoo, it's impossible to deny the resemblance. Every detail and line look ripped right from Hale's drawing.

The stranger doesn't seem to think so. He eyes the sketch skeptically, his mouth quirked. But he's wrong. Unless both men shared the same hallucination, Hale didn't dream this up on his own.

"What is that? Tell me!"

"No." He runs a hand over the skull and shrugs. Something about the motion seems forced, even as he flashes a grin. "It's nothing important, and we aren't here to talk. Hands up."

"No! Tell me what that means—"

"No." He snatches the pack from me and shoves it into his pocket. When I reach for it, he easily bats my hand away. "All this bitching and whining, but you don't even know the right questions to ask."

"My brother drew that," I rasp, unsure of what I've done to earn such a reaction from him. Something I said crossed a line. What? "Tell me what it means. Please."

"Later," he insists. "You give me what I want, first. You gonna hit me, or you afraid of breaking a nail?" He nods toward my hands.

I follow the line of his gaze, more confused than ever. I'm still wearing the pink nail polish I wore to Hale's funeral, reduced to peeling, messy chips. Ironically, he hated pink. In fact, he hated it when I painted my nails.

Father insisted on the manicure. I couldn't embarrass him by showing up ungroomed. It isn't until now that I parse over exactly what that meant—Hale was an embarrassment. Even in death, his wishes didn't matter.

"Hey!" The coarse shout draws my attention to the stranger. "No thinking," he snarls. "You want your shit back? Come and get it. Hit me! Or you gonna stand there crying like a little bitch?"

The vulgarity ignites something inside me.

"Fine!" I lunge forward and slam both hands into the mat. "Ow!" Instantly, I rear back, clutching my fingers to my chest.

They sting—but he didn't even flinch.

"Again," he commands, sinking into his stance—legs apart, shoulders up, head lowered. "And don't tuck your thumbs, unless you want to break them off. And bend your knees."

I obey him. So much for taking control of my life. Somehow, it's easier to let another person seize the figurative reins.

"No thinking," he snaps again. "Hit me—"

With a grunt, I swing, slapping the pad with both fists. Again. Again. "There!" Breathless, I'm shouting with every blow. "Are. You. Happy. Now?"

On the last attempt, I miss the pad entirely and wind up on my knees. My eyes burn, my vision blurring. When I swipe my hand across my face, it comes away wet.

"No, Blondie, I'm not happy."

Rather than gloating, he's across the room now. Abruptly, he tosses the mat aside and presses his hands against the wall, leaning forward. That simple motion distorts the tattoo on his back, and it's like the skeleton figure comes to life, glaring at me through hollow eye sockets.

"I'm not happy."

"No wonder," I counter softly. "If your only entertainment comes in the form of bothering strangers who are minding their own business—"

"Oh, shut the fuck up." The skeleton jumps with his next inhalation. Then he exhales, "You weren't going to jump."

Jump. It sounds so violent an action for what is, in essence, letting myself fall. "You don't know that."

"Like hell, I don't." Again, he laughs that arrogant laugh and spins to face me. "All you wanted was attention. Congrats. You fucking got it."

"What are you talking about?"

"You got *me*," he says in an ominous tone. "I'm sure you convinced yourself that no one would give a damn if they saw you up there. Well, sorry to break it to you, baby, I do."

"And who are you?" I toss back, genuinely unsettled by his taunt. "A stalker?"

He turns away rather than answer. With his shoulders hunched, I'm forced to acknowledge his size. He's huge. A wall of living, breathing muscle.

Someone, I don't have the energy to fight with, even verbally.

"Is this your gym?" I wonder, ignoring the obvious question lurking between us like a lit stick of dynamite. My brain won't let it go, however, dwelling on the potential connection between him and Hale. Did they know each other?

He whistles low. "You should really get out more often."

He doesn't want to play along. I stammer out another question anyway. "Springer doesn't seem like your part of town."

This place, on the other hand, does, just as jagged and rough as he is.

"I never took you for a snob, Blondie," he says, nothing more.

But I need more. More talking. More moving.

My raw nerves demand something—anything—as an outlet. It's either that or dwell. Dangerous memories flicker like wild electricity, daring me to relive them. Whether I like it or not, playing mind games with him is preferable.

"So why were *you* at the bridge?"

He chuckles, for real this time, and I catch myself staring. There's a calculated power in the way he speaks. Laughs. It's musical. Slow and rhythmic in places, but quick and pulsating in others. And yet, ruthlessly in sync.

"Do I really need to say it?" he asks. "Fine. I was sightseeing, Blondie—"

"Frey," I interject.

I've been absently touching the floor while observing him. This section has been worn down by countless scuffling feet. Brawls. Spars. It's like skin, wearing the weight of this building in a million tiny nicks and scratches most people wouldn't notice.

"Maybe you don't care, but my name's Frey."

"Well, Frey, I *don't* really care."

I shrug off his hostility. "So, what's yours?"

He's still leaning against the wall. Sweat rolls down the back of his neck, coating his hair and darkening the honey-blond strands.

"Jerk?" I quip, hazarding a guess. "Unrepentant Sinner? Corrupted Soul—"

"Close." God, that chuckle. It's rich and cold at the same time. Like a ghost of him is taunting me, but the real man's far away. "What the fuck does 'Frey' stand for anyway? Don't tell me your parents named you that."

"Yes," I snap. "It stands for 'none of your business.'"

"Well, 'none of your business,' the name's Daze."

I laugh at what has to be an obvious joke. "Really? You're making fun of my name when yours is *Daze*?"

"Hahaha. Laugh it up, sweetheart." His flat tone lacks the energy of real anger. More like he's going through the motions out of sheer habit. "Still better than Frey."

"Frances," I retort. "And I beg to differ."

"Whatever you say, Frey," Daze says under his breath. "Fuck. I'll be right back. I gotta wash this shit off me."

He disappears down a small hallway and emerges a few minutes later, drying his hands on a towel that he tosses aside. Holding my gaze, he reaches into his pants pocket and fishes out two loose cigarettes and a lighter. "I need a smoke."

Aware of me watching, he makes a spark and lights up one cigarette. After exhaling a grayish cloud, he cocks his head.

"You want one?"

I shake my head only for him to laugh that stupid laugh.

"I knew I had you pegged right." He clenches both cigarettes between his teeth.

"Pegged?" I can't resist glancing at my blue sweater, skirt, and sandals. For the first time, I consider the impression I must make on someone like him. Designer clothes. Unruly blond curls, ending just past my shoulders. Sandals in winter.

With an insufferably arrogant shrug, he flicks his lighter. After igniting the other cigarette, he withdraws them both. "With one look, I knew you were a goody goody."

"And I think you're on drugs," I counter childishly. "I know what sweating like that means, so don't lie."

I've been around Hale long enough to notice Daze's twitching hands and the sweat beading on his forehead. Addicts speak a nonverbal language, fluent in desperation.

Another reason to fear him.

Another warning I confusingly want to ignore.

"Are you?" I wonder boldly.

"Am I what?"

"On drugs."

I'm never like this. Callous. Rude. Probing. He's kryptonite to my polished, coddled persona—maybe that's it. Why I've stayed. Frances Heywood doesn't exist in this room. I'm bitchy little *Blondie,* left with no filter to hide behind.

And no escape from Hale. Memories of him fight their way out. I sense him in this room of all places. He'd love this. Somewhere dirty and dangerous, far from our father's control.

This man reminds me of him in the worst way. That could be the real reason why I've tolerated him this long.

It's a more fitting punishment than drowning.

"I'm sure you know every damn thing, Frey," Daze says. He clips my name between his teeth, sharpening the vowel.

"Tell me what that tattoo means." I nod to his chest, and it's as if an invisible curtain drapes his expression, instantly closing him off.

And I know for sure—he's avoiding the topic on purpose.

"Tell me—"

"I will," he says carefully. "But first, you tell me why you were at the bridge."

"I... I was walking," I stammer.

"Walking." He drags on his cigarettes and exhales, holding both between two fingers. The scent of smoke itches my nostrils, and I stifle a cough. "Like any bitchy little goody goody, you're a terrible liar."

I seethe at that assessment, but the "bitchy" part isn't what I take offense to. He makes "goody" sound synonymous with "irrelevant." As if all I am can be summed up in that one characterization.

Invisible.

"I'd believe you more if you said you were on your way to Bible study—"

"I changed my mind," I demand, cutting him off. "Give me a cigarette."

That startles him, and I take a savage glee in rattling his preconceived notions of me. Until I cough, that is. Still, I keep my palm outstretched.

"Say please." He wiggles his fingers, making the cigarettes dance. "Or come and get it."

It's obvious from his smirk what he thinks I'll do. Beg.

I take the dare instead, climbing to my feet. He evades me easily, shifting out of my reach with the grace of a dancer. The second time I snatch for the cigarette, he's ready for me, and puckered lips deliver a cloud of smoke directly into my face. Rather than cough, my lips part, letting in every cloying bit of air.

The action backfires. Sucking him down into my lungs only soothes the itch in my skin for a heartbeat. The moment I exhale, the pain returns like a slap, so raw it's crippling.

"What am I doing here?" I choke out. My knees buckle. The next second I'm on the floor, face in my hands, stomach clenching up into a knot.

"Alright, alright. Here." My wrist is snatched from above, a thin sliver of tobacco shoved between my fingers before I can react. He guides the butt to my mouth, and I see flames, lighting up the end.

"Inhale," Daze commands.

I do so slowly, relishing the burn of every ounce of tainted air over the tender flesh of my throat. I hold my breath so long my lungs protest, and it takes another order to get me to exhale.

"*Blow.*"

The moment I breathe out, a face comes into focus, gray-eyed and emotionless. Most people these days look at me with pity. He simply *looks* at me. I'm not sure which scrutiny is preferable.

Maybe it's him. I'm used to being gaped at, but no one else tempts me to stare back. Gawk.

He's older than I first thought. At least late twenties or early thirties. Tiny lines and wrinkles distort what once was boyish perfection, leaving him weathered. Hard. He's more worn out than the floor, and I can't stop myself from swiping my thumb against his chiseled jaw, feeling him for myself.

Ouch. He's not like I expect, as cold as concrete. He's softer. Burning.

"Why were you at the bridge?" I murmur. Maybe I really want to know. Or I just want the noise. Talking fills the silence, and suddenly that's all that matters. Blissful chatter where Hale's voice can't echo. "Were you really 'sightseeing'?"

He shakes his head but doesn't shrug off my touch. That emboldens me to add. "Your friend Ben made it sound like you're...involved in something dangerous." I'm still touching him, trailing my thumb down to the corner of his mouth. "He kept looking at me—"

"Now you're depressed *and* paranoid?" His eyes narrow, their color changing like the churning surface of the bay. I stare, both riveted and alarmed. He's unreadable one minute. Unbearable the next, brimming with emotion. Then he laughs, and all expression vanishes. He's empty again.

"Tell me something, *Frey,*" he says. "And don't lie to me. Your plan wasn't to jump. You wanted to cause a scene." He taps my chin in return, sliding the pad of his thumb over my skin.

"A what?" I ask, blinking innocently.

"Attention," he growls, finding the corner of my mouth— we're mirror images of each other now, and I can't recall a more perilous feeling.

My heart hammers like crazy, my skin on fire. No man has ever touched me like this. Ever.

But, a part of me scolds, *I touched him first.*

"Pretty little thing about to jump off a bridge. I bet you thought the whole world would stop and stare. That's what you wanted. To be fucking seen. But you should have questioned *who* might be watching."

He was. A man with blood on his hands who thinks I'm pretty.

"You want to know what I really want?" I ask him tiredly. "I don't want to talk. I don't want to be good. I want to do something bad. Like smoke."

"That request I can oblige." He rears back, a wicked grin shaping his lips. For the first time, I realize that he's on his knees, down to my level. I crane my neck to meet his gaze, and I'm left eyeing a square chin and broad nose that flares as he takes me in.

"Open," he commands after taking a drag of his lit cigarette.

The other cigarette trembles in my grasp. I've never smoked before in my life. Rather than lift it, I wait. When he exhales, my lips part, and I inhale him all the way down to the base of my lungs.

He smells good beneath the nicotine and blood. Like heat and strength and those weird intangible things young women aren't supposed to notice in men. Attraction is a foreign concept in my world. Lust is a sin. Even kissing Colton was flirting with a dangerous line. Father would kill me if he knew. He'd kill me twice if he knew I was here, committing a worse sin than Hale and his drugs ever could. Until marriage, my only worth lies in being a virgin, untouched and pristine.

But I don't feel clean. I feel so dirty I can't stand it.

"Stop being polite," Daze scolds. I flinch at his tone. It's like he's inside my head, scoffing at what he sees. "Just say why you're here. What you really fucking want from me."

"Answers," I blurt. "Tell me about the tattoo. Please. I mean... Now."

"Fine, but I doubt it means anything to someone like you." He dismissively eyes my skirt and sweater. "It's the symbol of the Saints. Ever heard of them?"

I blink, unsure if he's joking or not. "Like... Like the holy—"

"No, baby," he says with a laugh. "These Saints ain't gonna be found in your church books. They control the entire lower city. Just know that they're dangerous, and you don't need to know a damn thing more about them."

"Then why did my brother draw that?" I demand, pointing to the garish design.

He withdraws the drawing from his pocket and inspects it with an unreadable expression. Is that recognition in his eyes? It's driving me crazy that I can't tell.

"It was Hale's," I say, hoping to trigger a response. "I thought it was a random drawing at first—"

"But now you think I have something to do with it?"

I nod, feeling my chest tighten. His silence is torturous, lasting an eternity.

"I hate to break it to you, but it doesn't mean anything you'd understand—" He returns the pack to me. "He probably saw it on some graffiti."

"You didn't know him? His name was Hale."

He shakes his head. "Don't ring a bell. Now what?"

I should be used to pain and disappointment by now—but I'm not. Both suffocate me until I find myself blurting out, "I *really* want to forget."

"Oh?" He puts out his cig directly on the floor, leaving a mess of charred ashes and even more tufts of smoke. I sense him leaning closer, but he's hesitant, giving me more than enough time to turn away.

"There are plenty of men who might take that statement the wrong way," he says.

"Like how?"

Something unreadable flits across his gaze. "In ways a good girl like you would never consider."

His tone is neutral, but the subject is dangerous, one Colton and I rarely discussed, though not for lack of trying on his part. Sex was that scary, sacred thing I wasn't supposed to think about until marriage.

But now. With Daze...

Those dangerous thoughts I never entertained take on a greater, crueler significance. A good, rule-abiding person wouldn't let her brother die.

"Maybe I'm not good," I counter.

"Is that so?" He leans in as if daring me to flinch.

I don't.

He doesn't kiss me. He comes close enough to. Close enough for my lips to flutter in anticipation, still smarting from his smoke.

Mere centimeters away, he stills. "You're not my type."

His voice rasps. It's like he's trying to remind himself of that.

"What? Too blond?" I wonder, though, for some reason, I'm not insulted.

He wants an escape too, but I'm not his poison of choice. To prove it, he eyes me up and down, daring me to call him out.

"How old are you?" he asks, frowning.

"Twenty-three." I cock my head. "And what are you, like thirty? A bit too old to be hitting on random strangers."

As if I know the protocol for flirting. Colton was chosen for me, and I've never questioned our eventual union. I'm not even sure why I am now—but here we are.

"If I decided to flirt with a stranger, it wouldn't be you," I add.

That draws a chuckle from Daze, but it doesn't grate on my nerves like before.

"It's a good thing then that I'm not hitting on you. I'm not kissing you, either," he says more seriously.

"Good." I scoff. I'm still not offended. I'm not. "Because I wouldn't—"

Skin. Contact. Heat. I don't realize it's his teeth my tongue is pressed against until I taste him. Messy. Sloppy. Open.

We're miss-matched and uncoordinated, worse than even my first childhood kiss under the swing set in Nanna's backyard. Right when I accidentally bite his tongue, he breaks away, chuckling.

"No offense. But you're a fucking terrible kisser." But a smile shapes his lips and...

It's so *broken*. Like he's only half here, with the rest of him far away again, chasing some invisible high. All I can do is remember my still burning cigarette, and I inhale from the end. Maybe I'm imagining things, but he's looking at me again. *Really* looking. So I keep smoking even as my eyes water. For some reason, his attention seems worth the discomfort.

"So tell me, Blondie. You've stuck around this long. Why?"

The question comes just as I choke out another cloud of smoke. Frowning, I watch the tufts drift and fade.

It's so quiet here. There's just the two of us in this whole building. Two bodies trapped within yards and yards of space. Every move echoes. Every breath. Every sigh.

Every bit of hesitation.

"Do you mean here with you?" I finally question. "Or here in general—"

"Don't play dumb." He's impatient again. Clarity in him comes and goes, but when it returns, it's like bursts of heat against frostbitten skin, worse than the entire congregation's judgment.

"Would you believe I'd rather not be alone?" I eye my fingers rather than observe him directly. "I was supposed to be volunteering this morning. Pretending like everything is better, and my brother isn't dead."

Despite eyeing my nails, I sense him stiffen.

"So rather than hug the homeless or whatever it is you people do, you decided to kill yourself?"

He's not mocking me anymore. My skin feels itchy beneath his judgment, like a suit that's too tight. Hale hated wearing them. He loathed getting dressed up in general—mainly because of what it meant. Another dinner. Another event. Another charade to pretend and smile.

In his casket, however, he wore a tailored black one Father picked out. Black wasn't even his favorite color.

Blue was.

"What else was I supposed to do?" I inquire out loud. Tears prickle at my eyes, but by the time I rub at them, it's too late.

More beads of moisture escape my fingers and paint my cheeks.

I wait a few more seconds before I realize that Daze doesn't have an answer.

"And you?" I ask rudely. "Why were you there so early? You can't tell me anything?"

I'm shamelessly prying, but it's only fair. An eye for an eye. Lately, I've been so wrapped up in myself, I barely remember what it feels like to listen and not scream. To wait in silence while someone else weighs their answers. It's annoying. No wonder so many people ignore me.

But for some reason, I can't ignore him.

"We can start with why you're in a gang." I nod to his neck tattoo.

"A gang," he parrots coldly. "But you don't seem afraid."

Deep down, I know I should be.

"What the hell do you even know about a *gang*?" Daze shifts just enough to ram his shoulder into mine. It's not a violent gesture, at least I don't think, but he's so damn huge. My entire body shifts as he settles next to me.

"I know you look like you could be a criminal," I point out, rubbing my arm. "Considering the blood on your clothes."

His jaw clenches, and he cuts his gaze to the wall beyond me. "It's paint," he grunts. "And, baby girl, I don't think you'd know a criminal if one pissed on your shoe."

I curl my toes. "Don't tell me that's your next move?"

He laughs. "Let's say I *was* in a gang. You wouldn't understand." His voice... It's too deep now, rumbling in my bones. "You wouldn't know what it's like to believe in something beyond yourself. To have no choice. You're either in or out, and if you're out, you're as good as dead."

"Like a church?" I ask.

Or something worse? Something so powerful the only way out is to jump off a bridge?

He nods. "Exactly like that. Only the head of *this* organization takes his marching orders from the devil. Believe it or not, it wasn't always that way..." He stares off into the distance, glowering at a fragment of his past I can't see.

I should say something nice. Something supportive, like a normal person would. That fake, superficial brand of sympathy the rest of the world seems to enjoy dishing out.

Instead...

I sigh and take a page out of his playbook. "So, you'd rather kill yourself than go to therapy?"

"Right." He looks at me funny—a single jab from the corner of his eye. Then he tilts his head back, causing his hair to spill around his shoulders.

"If you really aren't in some kind of gang, then you should get a haircut," I tell him ruefully.

Father would certainly think so. He'd sneer down that perfect, Romanesque nose and declare as much. But somehow, it would seem more like a kind suggestion rather than an insult.

It was his superpower of sorts—kindness utilized as a weapon.

"You think you can give *me* advice on hair?" His fingers, heavy and rough, land on my head without warning. Heedless of how I flinch, he rakes through a curl. "Bullshit. And I suppose next you're gonna advise me on my fashion choices?" He tugs on my sleeve. "You can keep that fucking advice."

"You're right." I look down at my sweater.

Wearing it is starting to feel more painful than nostalgic. It's like a part of Hale lives within the material. Haunting me. Hating me.

Blaming me.

"You're right," I repeat.

I don't think the indecency through as I curl my fingers around the hem of my top. I just lift, wrenching it over my head. The thin undershirt I have on beneath feels like tissue paper, unable to withstand his scrutiny.

He doesn't say a word to stop me, though. He watches me crumble the colorful garment into a ball and throw it as hard as I can.

My eyes are burning again, too fiercely to soothe by just blinking. I smash my palms over them, physically shoving back anything that might fall. One second. Two. It's enough for now. I don't feel anything on my face but warm bursts of air, each punctuated by a hollow laugh.

"Look at me," he dares.

"No." A part of me wants to stick out my tongue. Deny him. Rebel.

I'm so tired of pretending to be good, old Frey. The girl who doesn't blink when you say boo. The girl who always minds her Ps and Qs.

The girl who knows her father's dirty little secrets without spilling a word.

I can't be her again.

But...

"Look at me."

There's something about his voice. It's too soft. If stone talked, it would sound like him, deceptively quiet, but with enough strength in every syllable to hurt. Move mountains. Make me listen.

"Come on. *Look* at me."

I spread my fingers apart. From this angle, a shadow falls over his face, rendering it unreadable. Just haunting eyes and a wistful frown. Even so, there is a strange beauty hidden within the gruff features. Or maybe I'm fooling myself simply because he isn't scolding me?

Unlike everyone else in my life, he doesn't seem concerned for my soul—or anything for that matter.

"What are you thinking about?" he wonders, watching me in silence while I wait for the punchline to land. He'll laugh next, snicker, or make some snide joke to negate any real concern. No one ever means that question.

So, I wait, and I wait.

Until he finally scoffs, kicking one of his heels against the floor. "You that damn paranoid, Frey?"

I wince at the insinuation. "No. I just... I'm thinking about whether or not 'rock bottom' is when you're sitting next to a stranger in an empty room with no shirt on."

"No. I've been lower." He sounds way too grim.

To distract myself, I pose another question, picked at random. "There was blood on your hands before. Are you an escaped convict?"

"I ain't *escaped*. They let me out for good behavior."

"Oh..." I suck in air and release it through clenched teeth. It's harder to decipher whether he's joking or telling the truth. "Did you do your time for murder or petty theft?"

I sound like I'm joking.

But he's not. His eyes tell me everything I need to know.

"All of the above, sweetheart. You're doing that thing again, by the way."

"What thing?" Confused, I look up to catch him staring.

"Wandering off. Daydreaming isn't productive, you know. I

bet you're imagining how I look naked or some shit. Hate to break it to ya, but you couldn't handle it—"

"You're right," I admit. "I am imagining how you'd look naked. You might have even more gang tattoos."

"Touché." His wince tells me I hit a soft spot. "And I bet you, on the other hand, don't have a mark on you. Nothing to explain why you were standing on the edge of a bridge."

"Maybe..." I lick my lips to find enough traction to keep talking. "Maybe I wasn't going to jump."

I don't know where the admission comes from. I could be feeding off his bravado, though it could be something about how damn bluntly he speaks. The man has no filter, and I find that mine is being worn away the longer I humor him.

"I can't swim," I admit.

"Which is kind of the point," he says, teasing. I think, anyway.

His lips quirk up into the shadow of a smile. My stomach squirms the longer I stare, and I'm realizing that I don't like the feeling. Just like everything else about him, his smile comes without warning, gone in a flash. I only have a second to judge it—way too pretty for a tattooed guy to possess.

"Someone like you, I wonder why you didn't just overdose?" he adds. "You look like a rich little princess. I'm sure you have access to the right pills."

Like the painkillers my stepmother keeps in the master bathroom medicine cabinet.

My teeth sink into my lower lip to combat the sharp, prickling sensation creeping behind my eyelids. "Hale overdosed," I hear myself croak.

I think the coroner's report officially read "respiratory distress," but that wasn't it. No. Hale's veins got injected with lies, fed to his heart until it finally stopped beating.

"I don't know what happened. He used to hate drugs. Our Mom..." I trail off and shake my head. "He was a sponsor, you know? For addicts. He did a lot of work on behalf of the church. He volunteered at our outreach program. He was so... Good. Everyone thought he was perfect."

I certainly did.

"He *was* perfect..."

"Hey. Earth to Frey."

I blink, yanked back to the present. Daze is eyeing me again, his smile gone, his expression almost serious. For all his tough talk, he doesn't like being ignored. He gives himself away in little moments like this, reminding me of a guy at a bar constantly demanding a stream of booze. *Keep it coming,* he'd beg the bartender. Talking is like that for him. A vice.

"I heard what your friend, Ben, told you," I say. "Maybe you're not my knight in shining armor, after all? You're just trying to distract yourself from your own problems."

He scoffs, eyeing the floor. "That so?"

"Was he in your gang?" I wonder, aimlessly probing for a nerve to strike. He stiffens—I've hit the jackpot. "Let me guess. You were some kind of bigshot and then got busted. Now you atone for your sins by taunting suicidal women out of jumping from bridges."

"Something like that." He sighs, shaking his head. "But being in charge ain't all it's cracked up to be."

"Tell that to Father."

"Damn, girl. You've got daddy issues, alright."

"What does that even mean?"

He faces me head-on, his eyes piercing. "It means that a guy could get the wrong idea."

He keeps saying that.

"Maybe," I admit. "If this was some cheesy afterschool special."

Not that I'm an expert in those. I wasn't allowed to watch cable at home, and my only experience in popular dramas came from gossip or whatever movies I caught while out with friends. Even after I graduated, my diet of pop culture has been sparse.

Drawing on the knowledge of those plots, I try to play along. "Is this the part where you tell me that I'm the prettiest girl you've ever seen, and that we should get out of here and go somewhere private—"

"To do what?" he says innocently, rubbing his chin. He reaches out and thumbs the golden cross hanging from my neck. "Read a Bible?"

"To, well…" I shrug him off and sigh. "Colton calls it 'holding hands.'"

I wince for a multitude of reasons. I've never felt anything for Colton, and a part of me has always wondered why Father can't see that. Why in his mind, we're together. He's already jumped to the obvious conclusion that we'll be married by the year's end despite no announcement on my part. Although, after he dismissed Hale's feelings so easily, I'm starting to wonder if Father has ever truly cared about us at all.

What *we* want.

"Interesting." Daze's voice drops an octave. "Who's Colton?"

"No-nobody," I stammer. "He's nobody."

"Well, I've got a psychotherapy question for ya," he proposes, crossing his arms. "What's more self-destructive, *Freylie* Frey? Killing yourself or spilling your guts out to a stranger?"

"Spilling my guts," I admit. "I'm not used to talking to anyone. Not like this."

Except maybe Hale, once upon a time.

"Not even your boyfriend, Colton?" he prods.

"It's not what you think. He's not my boyfriend. I mean, Colton is beautiful and nice, and perfect. But we aren't together. I'm just expected to end up with him. I don't have any say."

It sounds so strange when spelled out. Daze's bemused smirk confounds my unease.

"I was wrong," he says softly. "You have more than just Daddy issues. It sounds like you have 'Colton' issues, too. And what am I? The big bad monster you play with for a little while before running back to their safe harbor?"

"I didn't ask you to save me," I snap. Then my ears burn as my word choice echoes in an endless loop.

Save me. Save me.

"I'm not complaining," he says. "Use me all you want. I'll be your monster."

The words should sound mocking. In his grated monotone, they just sound...

Like a plea.

"You never told me why you were at the bridge," I say. "Which is more self-destructive? Talking to me or pretending that you weren't covered in blood earlier?"

"First, you tell me. Which is worse? Returning to your perfect life right now or being denied my secrets a little while longer?"

"I'm tired of being lied to," I admit tiredly. "By Hale. Father. I'm tired of lying."

His lips quirk, but into less of a smile. More like a grimace. "So if I *did* know your brother, and *if* there was something more to that drawing, would it even matter?"

It could be a hypothetical question, but no... His voice is too deep. Pensive.

"Yes," I insist. "Of course, it would. And I would want you to tell me."

He grunts. "Doesn't answer my question. But to answer yours... Pretending is way more self-destructive. I don't think you could hurt me if you wanted to."

His tone alone dares me to reach out with two fingers and seize a sliver of skin on his forearm. I pinch him hard.

He doesn't even wince. "You see? Now my turn." He touches my forearm but doesn't pinch. His heat burns just as painfully, though. "What's the worst thing you could do right now to make this all worth it before you run back to your father... and Colton?"

"What do you mean?"

He shrugs. "You're the one on a self-destructive vendetta. Not me."

There are several things, but one sticks out in my mind the most. Any other time, I'd never have the nerve to voice it. It's so crazy. So reckless.

"The worst thing I could do? Kiss some weird stranger in a random alley and wallow in my descent to rock bottom."

"Just a kiss? Don't be a girl scout. I'm sure you can think of worse than that."

He's right. This dilemma requires careful consideration, so I copy his posture. Looking at him, I come up with the answer as my gaze traces his broad, hard form.

"Sex." I shiver just saying it. I never talk like this. Ever. "But a girl would have to be pretty pathetic. Especially if the guy was a weird stranger."

"And the guy?" Daze pitches in. "Well, he'd have to be one desperate motherfucker. I mean, he could go pick up something harsher on the street. Some good blow that might last a few days, at least. But some girl? She'd probably distract him for ten minutes, tops. Five if she has no tits."

A sound trickles out of me that I don't recognize at first. Frowning, I try to decipher it. A laugh, maybe? One more genuine than any before it. The kind of giggle I haven't heard in months. Or years. My arms are around my chest again before I realize it, as if the added protection can lock any other emotions inside.

"Yeah," I whisper. "Pretty desperate."

"So maybe I should cut to the chase?" I stiffen as he props an elbow on his knee. "I'm desperate. You're pathetic. We're both here, where I happen to keep a stash of the cheapest, chaffiest condoms known to man. Want to have probably terrible, impersonal sex to further avoid our personal shit for at least an hour longer?"

He doesn't laugh. His lips don't even quirk into the faintest hint of a smile. He's more serious now than when he dragged me off a bridge. And deep down in the pit of my stomach, I know the answer he wants to hear. The answer a normal, sane person would give.

No.

But in the absence of jumping off a bridge, he might be the next best thing, as sick as that may be. A punishment I deserve—to become the person Hale thought I was. Broken and dirty.

Unluckily for us both, I think Daze is tailor-made to indulge my worst rebellious inclinations.

I deserve it.

I deserve so much worse than this.

"Do you want to sleep together, Daze?" I ask, feeling my cheeks catch fire despite the bravado my voice conveys.

He holds my gaze ruthlessly, unwilling to shy from the suggestion. "You mean *fuck*?"

I know I'm blushing harder than ever, but I manage to nod anyway.

He just sighs, like someone gearing up for another hit from the easiest vice within reach. When his voice finally echoes off the walls, he sounds more exhausted than I feel. "Okay."

FIVE

NO ONE'S ever looked at me the way *he* does. Like he's missing nothing. Not the freckles on my collar bone or the protruding ribs.

It's too much attention. Too much scrutiny.

"I won't bite," he taunts. I've been staring at him this whole time.

He can see everything above my shoulders and a sliver of what peeks above my undershirt. I should keep it that way, hoarding as much of myself from him as I can. I should leave. Remember my duty as dictated by my father to stay pure for my future husband.

But where is the self-destruction in that?

Daze's right. A vengeful vendetta has more appeal than continuing to grieve in silence. Though, to his credit, he seems willing to offer me an out.

"We were joking," he adds playfully, raising his hands in defeat. "Hypothetically, if you fuck like you kiss, I doubt I'm missing much."

But he's already laid down the dare, and before doubt can set in, I let my hands fall, watching his nostrils flare at the sight. It's like he's reading every thought in my head, hating the conclusion I come to. Daze the druggie. What a catch.

"Or not?" he taunts, his voice dangerously soft.

Gritting my teeth, I remove my undershirt first. Next, I finger the fastenings of my skirt, but I'm not brave enough to gauge his reaction. Instead, I face the opposite wall as I drag it down my legs, my chest heaving. It's cold in here, but I don't feel it, even as my breaths paint the air before me white. I'm disconnected from my body, just a ghost inhabiting a shell.

Or so I think. That aching feeling in the pit of my stomach growing with every passing second of silence might be shame. Desperate, I try to ignore it.

But he doesn't seem eager to help me. He's still seated on the floor, just watching.

"Are we doing this or what?" I croak without turning around. My hands still shake, and fisting them through my hair is the only way I can disguise it. "Now you don't want to talk?"

Finally, the floor trembles with movement, but his steps are heavy. Slow. Reluctant? It's impossible to gauge just where he is. Close?

Closer. A gasp rips from my throat as his hand finally brushes my hip. My gaze darts to it, watching each finger spread out to cover as much flesh as he can in one go.

"Last chance," he warns in an alarmingly soft rumble. Too soft. My eyes drift shut as if to capture the feeling of how he said it. Maybe this will make it easier to punish myself later? I'll hear his voice and remember this fall to rock bottom. "Just say the word, Frey—"

"Stop talking."

He does, and no warning comes as he spins me around. I inhale as his breath floods my lungs, rich with coffee, sweat, and cigarettes. One inhalation isn't enough to decipher him completely.

There's something raw lurking underneath the over-whelming flavor of him, and my tongue latches onto the spicy tang. Desperation? Loathing? Self-hate?

He's like a mirror, reflecting every emotion I don't want to feel. Things that are so easy to ignore with anyone else. *Bad sign*, some inner voice warns, but it's no louder than a whisper.

Daze's presence easily drowns it out. He's still holding me captive, sliding his hand up to my cheek. My stomach bunches into knots as heat flares along my skin. A shift in the air is my only warning before I feel his lips brush my own, demanding to be let in. I open my mouth on instinct, only to feel nothing.

"Slow down." I feel him speak the words against my tongue. His other hand cups the side of my jaw, guiding my head to a position he approves of. "Look at me."

No, that little voice inside me warns. But it's no use. My eyelids flutter, revealing his face in blurred snippets. Stern frown. Mockingly raised eyebrow. Dangerous tongue still sliding along his lower lip, capturing my taste.

"Close your lips," he tells me, nudging my bottom one until I comply. "Yeah, like that. Now *feel*. We can go slow. I'm not in any damn rush."

Slow. My heart doesn't like that word. It panics, sending my pulse surging. I feel it throbbing through my fingertips, making them twitch even more. I have to ball both hands into fists to stop it.

Slow. Patience is the weapon he uses to pry my mouth open with deliberate flicks of his tongue. Like he has all of time at his disposal. Time to waste away fucking a stranger in his shitty gym. Time to taste her. Smell her—he's sloppy when he's sensing me. I can hear every deliberate, thieving inhale. That's what he does—steals, taking away pieces of me to pore over later.

It's more invasive than sex—one violation I didn't sign up for.

"Don't fight me," he warns between those devious lashes of his tongue. "Let me in. *This* is how you kiss, Freylie Frey."

This. Slow, sensual bursts. Rough, searing nudges. Grating teeth. Blistering heat.

All.

At.

Once.

I've barely wrapped my mind around it all when I feel his hands slide down to my shoulders. Then lower. One brush of my breast makes my nipple react, and the resulting sensations twist my stomach into knots.

Too much.

Too fast.

He's soft when he wants to be. Harsh when he doesn't. Raking nails draw a gasp that he swallows whole. Then that searching hand lowers while more fingers sink into my hair, locking my head in place.

"Trust me," he murmurs. Or more like nibbles against my tongue in a series of sharp little bites.

"Let's just do this," I stammer, pulling back. "I don't want romance. I just want..." Aimlessly, I head for a nearby corner containing a table stacked with random equipment. The distance from him doesn't help clear my mind any.

It only reinforces why I'm here. Not for comfort. Just...pain. My heart hammers, my throat dry. I'm more desperate for a distraction than ever. In a sick way, I've gotten my wish—being alone with him is more disconcerting than standing on the edge of a bridge.

"If you want to leave—" Daze starts.

I shake my head. Unlike before, I'm ready to jump. "Where are your condoms?" I ask in a trembling voice.

"I have one," he says. From where? I didn't hear him leave the room, but I'm too chicken to ask.

My brain is too busy spouting its own questions, but they're directed at me. *What are you doing, Frey?*

I'm not ready when his thumb captures my chin, tilting it as if to second that question. He doesn't make me look at him, but I sense it's deliberate—his way of giving me an out. He's softer than he should be, manipulating flesh and bone without seeming to try. Those bruised, battered fingers promise damage that his touch alone seems incapable of delivering, and I shudder, releasing a breath I didn't even realize I was holding.

Another brush of his thumb demands I move closer. Close enough for my bare back to graze his chest, sending a jolt of alarm through my belly. Raw skin. Body heat. I'm feeling every sensation more than I have in weeks. Months. Even his scent sinks too deep, imprinting his presence inside my skull.

But something warns me I'll remember this one—my first descent to rock bottom.

I can feel every crushing ounce of the fall for once. His fingers mainly, sliding against my inner thigh, slow and hesitant. But bold too. Sure. I know this kind of touch. To him, I'm not a person in this moment. Just a cigarette he's dragging on, too desperate for a hit to care about the long-term consequences. Fuck lung cancer. Or logic. Or common sense that warns of all the risks that come from sleeping with a stranger...

I cringe from the reality, too, squeezing my eyes shut as my hands find the nearest stable surface. A table? It creaks as I brace myself against it, leaning away from him.

In return, he follows me, dominating me from behind. Hell-fire heat returns. Thick, immoveable muscle everywhere. A hitch catches in my throat, and a noise bubbles from it. Hesitation?

He doesn't give me the benefit of the doubt. Voice rasping, he warns, "You want me to stop—you tell me to stop." At the same time, his hand curves so that he has my entire thigh in his grasp. He lifts it easily, spreading my legs apart, opening me up to him. Gingerly, he hooks a thumb beneath the waistband of my panties and tugs them down.

My heart hammers against my ribcage, and I can't help but compare him to Colton. Beautiful, brown-eyed Colton with the rich, donating father who supports Father in money and a presence at the church.

The boy I'm expected to one day marry.

You're the most beautiful girl in the world, Frey, he told me.

Daze inhales when he sees me, or so I presume, but it's a frantic sound. Impatient and hollow. I'm ruining his high with silence again. "Do you want me to stop, or—"

"No." I shake my head, resisting the fear. The memories. Everything. I'm cold, empty Frey again. Gritting my teeth, I wiggle my hips, seeking him out. "Just do it."

But he evades me.

"You're not even wet." Something he knows firsthand as what feels like his thumb slips between my legs. I jolt forward, electrified, and scrape my nails against the surface beneath them. I want to be carefree, stupid, and reckless, but panic floods my chest, and I'm suffocating again.

Focus, Frey. Focus, focus, focus. It's either this or Hale. Hale, Hale, Hale. You failed him—

"Why does that matter?" I choke out, trying to bat his hand away.

"I want to fuck you," he admits gruffly, evading my attempts to stop him. "But I don't want to hump a sex doll. Just relax..."

My breath hitches as I realize what he's doing. Stroking. The pad of his thumb is calloused, catching at tender flesh with every swipe. It feels...

I shake my head, resisting the urge to describe it. I want mindless oblivion. The opposite of what it felt like when Colton insisted on kissing me.

"Stop thinking," Daze scolds as if reading my mind again. He crooks his finger, sowing more friction with every stroke. "Good... Let yourself feel."

Feel. My thoughts dissipate, and I have to look down to realize what he's done—eased one of his fingers inside me. Out. Inside. Deeper.

My cheeks burn at the image. His hand, my skin. My eyes water. It's the most vulgar sight I've ever seen, etched in my memory more than any ghosts from the past.

I can't tell if it's a good feeling or bad.

But I don't fight it either.

"Good girl," Daze grunts when I fall silent. "I won't hurt you. You can trust that I at least know how to fuck."

Fuck. It should be mindless. Grunting and thrusting. Sharp pain. Panting.

Then nothing. And shame. And loathing. Self-hate. And...

I can't remember. I can't think at all anymore. His voice slithers into my head, drowning out everything else.

"Fuck, you're tight," he hisses.

Is that a good thing? Bad thing?

Very bad, I realize as warmth brushes my shoulder. His mouth?

"Don't tell me you're a virgin," he breathes against my ear.

I can't even get the answer out. *Yes.*

Another finger—two inside me at once. It hurts. Should it? My flesh stings, stretched beyond reason, and I flinch, squirming against the intrusion.

"Easy, baby." He sucks in a breath, and his touch softens. "Hell, you're *too* tight—"

I whimper.

"I gotta get you ready for me, or this won't work—"

"Okay," I manage to croak.

I can't tell if he hears me or not. I'm too busy registering how he feels. Different from the horror stories I've been told. I don't feel ruined. I feel...full. Those cigarettes must have been laced with something stronger than nicotine. My head is spinning, thoughts dissipating.

And then his fingers curl and...

"God!" My entire body jolts against him. I see stars, and it's too much. I buck away as he aims for the same spot again. "Too much—"

"You need to come at least once," he warns—but he doesn't make it sound romantic and mythical like most men do. Not a gift but a necessity. "I've got you."

He's closer than before. A mass of solid heat throbs against my hip.

"I need you wet," he says thickly as if reading my mind. "Trust me."

Trust. But that's beyond my expertise. All I can do is lean against the surface supporting me, and breathe. I can't even begin to describe what he does with his fingers. Pushes, pulls, takes. Harder. Harsher.

"So much for that smart fucking mouth," Daze rasps against my ear. A taunt? "Come on, Freylie. Move those lips. Tell me how to get you off. Is *this* the spot?"

His fingers slam into me, going even deeper. My throat clenches around a throaty sound I barely recognize as coming from me.

"No?" Daze murmurs, chuckling. I swear I feel his teeth nip at my earlobe as he eases those fingers out of me. Then he thrusts them again, even deeper, firmly stroking my walls. "Come on, Freylie. Get out of your head. Get out of your head and just *feel*."

And the second I do... Everything changes.

I push away all my worries, so I don't have a single care in the entire universe, and feel *everything*. Every touch. Every breath. Every sensation.

"What about here?" he asks, sinking his fingers deeper. "Or... here?"

More white stars twinkle behind my eyelids. My breaths come in pants, my voice echoing back to me, high-pitched. A stranger's.

"Yeah," Daze says, sounding alarmingly clear even as the rest of the world seems to fall away. "Here—" He thrusts again, and nerves I didn't even know existed ignite. Gritting my teeth doesn't lock in the moan that rips from me. "God, you're fucking sexy. You should get out of that pretty little head of yours more often."

He groans, forging a rhythm that sends the surface beneath us rocking back and forth with every motion. It's like burning alive. I can't stop it. Can't resist it. My muscles tighten up with every bold, prodding touch until...

"Holy crap!" I slump forward as every muscle inside me tightens even more, and then he flexes his fingers, and I finally realize what he means.

Wet. An overwhelming mixture of tension and pleasure that spills over, impossible to contain. Growing up, I was always taught that being intimate with a man before marriage was a sin. That casual sex was dirty. That it would result in no pleasure.

Except, I'm just now realizing that they were wrong.

So undoubtedly wrong.

How could this be?

"Are you still here with me, Frey?" he asks.

"Yes," I faintly reply.

"Good girl," he praises, his voice ragged. "Now get ready. I'll try to go slow, but fuck. It's been a while…"

Which must be why his hands shake as he positions me against him. Fabric hisses, and the sensation against the back of my thighs shifts from thick cotton to…skin. Fire. Sweat. He fumbles with something, presumably the condom. And then I feel him, settling between my legs, his breathing harsh against my spine.

Inch by inch, he drives into me slowly. Taking my bottom lip between my teeth, I attempt to stifle my pain. Squeezing my eyes shut, I grip the edge of the table until my knuckles turn white.

"Fucking hell," he breathes sharply, my inner walls gripping him tightly.

My body is like a fist around him. I don't think it's even

possible for him to move until he does anyway. An inch. More. More. More.

It hurts. I've never felt so *full*. So stretched.

So alive...

"Breathe," he instructs, almost sensing my discomfort as my body tries to accommodate his size.

Inhale.

"Good," he rasps, drawing back slightly before sinking into me further. "Frey—Did I just—"

Take my virginity?

Exhale. "Yes."

He suddenly becomes still, as if second-guessing everything.

I, however, am not. I've never been so sure about anything in my life. This is my body. My choice. Nobody else gets to decide when and where... and who.

I do.

Self-destructive vendetta or not.

"Frey," he questions, brushing my hair to the side, exposing my neck.

"I want this," I tell him. "Please."

He grasps my hips, his breathing now shallow.

Again and again, he moves within me, bringing me closer.

"Is this okay?" he asks carefully.

"Yes," I murmur.

My head rears back against his shoulder as a stranger's moan reverberates throughout the room. Me? A low, guttural sound like the rev of a jet engine follows it.

This isn't fucking.

This is taking. A high so intense I can't lie still beneath it, a slave to the pleasure. I writhe instead, resisting the pull. Too weak to keep it from dragging me under.

The pain turns to pure pleasure, an intense feeling of sensations that I've never felt before.

And somehow, he knows.

"Good girl. You can take it. All of me...like that..." He bucks into me with no reprieve. Slow and steady. "Take all of me, Frey." Then harder, slamming in, drawing out screams. Moans. Cries. "Fuck, I can't..." His fingers curl in my hair, forcing my head back as his mouth finds my ear. "Oh, fuck..."

He slams home, holding himself deep as I fall apart.

SIX

I'M NO EXPERT, but I thought destruction would feel far worse than this...

Shouldn't it?

Rather than burn in hellfire for all eternity, we wind up lying on the black mat, dripping sweat. Our bodies dominate opposite ends, not touching but still too close. Close enough to sense his breathing slow and hear how his teeth click together when he can't stay silent anymore.

"You stood at that railing for well over half an hour." His tone is softer, either from exhaustion or pity. Gone is the raspy hum—he's serious. "I *watched* you."

That statement sends a quiver through my belly.

I shift, crossing my arms over my chest. "How do you—"

"I wasn't going to let you jump." He laughs darkly, shaking his head. "Why do it anyway? Did you want to feel it? Falling? Crashing? The pain?"

He rolls to face me. Both of his legs unfold before him, nearly twice the length of mine. He's so big in such an enclosed space. Too big to jump off a bridge unnoticed. I'd barely make a splash, but he'd make waves falling from that height.

"Did *you*? Why else were you there?" I don't look at him as I pose the question. So many stains, mysterious and dark, speckle the gray concrete floor around the mat. Blood? Sweat? Spit? The material doesn't reveal any answers when I swipe my palm against it. Just cold, hard silence.

"Maybe," he says finally. He sounds heavy when he's being honest—a weird thing to notice after knowing someone for barely an hour. He's cyclic, spitting out truth and lies in an almost predictable rhythm. His lies are soft and empty, but the truth lands like a sucker punch.

And the sting makes me feel something. Even if it's pain.

"I'll tell you what, though. If I were going to off myself, I wouldn't want to fucking feel it," he says. He lifts his arm above him, eyeing the tattoos painting his skin from wrist to shoulder. "I'd go numb. Get high, so I wouldn't have to feel shit. Not the guilt or regret..."

He trails off, but the confession isn't for me. In a way, he's speaking for both of us, deploying a rare, potent drug. Honesty. My veins hum, gobbling it up, sending it straight through my heart. I'm not addicted, but it's only a matter of time.

I might be just as susceptible to vices as Hale. We shared a mother, after all.

"My...brother. He was the best person you could ever meet. I mean it," I hear myself confess, but I don't really register saying the words. More than anything else, it's like my thoughts are spilling out into the open—all those dirty things I'd never say to anyone else. "But then he changed. Hale knew something. Something bad. He wanted to tell. He tried to tell me, I think..."

But I was too selfish to listen. *Father isn't the savior he pretends to be,* Hale ranted to me once. *What's really going on? It's bad, Frey. It's bad.*

Not long after, he ended up dead.

Daze should react just like everyone else. Roll his eyes and tell me I'm foolish. Dramatic. Paranoid.

I've heard it all before.

"That fucking sucks, Blondie," he bellows on a sigh, so heavy. So real. He's not joking now. Instead, he kicks his heels against the floor, sending up tiny waves of dust. "That fucking sucks..."

"So, what now?" I gesture between us with a trembling hand. "Do we hold hands? Pray? Do you cut and run?"

I insisted Colton do the first two options when he made us kiss.

"I could," he says, nodding. Sweat glues his hair to his shoulders, and I lose track of the conversation the longer I stare. God, the man is a canvas of tattoos. In addition to the artwork on his back, his chest is a collage of skulls and letters. Names.

"Samuel," I read, too curious to keep from reaching out to finger the name written on the center of his chest, right over his heart. "Someone I should know about?"

He brushes my hand aside. "Don't tell me *you're* the one wanting to cut and run. Don't go hunting for shit to get upset over." He sighs and rolls onto his back, eyeing the ceiling. "You want to leave—you leave. You want to stay—you stay."

Hunting. Is that what I'm doing? I eye my outstretched fingers and curl them one by one into a fist. Then I shift to copy him, lying on my back.

I don't know how long we lie like this.

Too long.

My eyes are fluttering open when I regain my senses again. Alarm slams into me, making me scramble upright. Did I fall asleep?

I did…and he's still sleeping. God, it's so unfair for someone so abrasive to be so beautiful. Ignore the sweat and grime, and his body could be an exhibit in some weird art gallery focusing on tattoos. I start to touch one—an intricate design spanning his hip—only to stop myself halfway. My finger trembles inches from his skin before I finally force myself to bridge the gap and touch him.

I'm already too far gone to start using my common sense now. Rock meet bottom.

I trace the design with the tip of my nail, following the curves up and around to the flat of his stomach. Then down, grazing his pelvis. It isn't long before I realize that he isn't sleeping anymore—at least, one part of his anatomy is very much awake. He's so big. *Thick*. I try to ignore it, teasing his skin like a game of hide and seek. The longer I explore, the easier it is to escape logic, panic, and the ache between my legs demanding I remember what he felt like inside me.

I switch to another tattoo over his ribcage, but as I crest the ridge of his chest, I notice that a pair of gray eyes are intently watching my every move. The moment our gazes connect, he grabs my wrist, pulling my hand away.

"Damn, girl," he says thickly.

It's strange how those two words convey more than most people I know can say in a million meaningless sentences. *Damn, it's early. Damn, I'm tired. Damn...you're pushing me too far.*

He tugs until I settle down beside him. "It sounds like the world's ending out there."

"Huh?"

He inclines his head to the nearest wall. "Listen."

I strain my ears and catch the hint of police sirens and wailing firetrucks. Strange. I'd been so wrapped up in his body that I didn't even notice.

"It's probably an accident," Daze says. He still has my wrist in his grasp, and lifts it, observing my fingers and the thin bones in my wrist. "Either that or you got way more attention than you bargained for, Princess. Your rich father probably sent out the swat team, looking for you."

I swallow hard, alarmed by how accurately he has me pinned down just from a few snippets of information. *I watched you,* he said, referring to how long I stood at the bridge. But what if he meant longer?

No. I shake my head, pushing the thoughts away. *I'm being paranoid.*

"Maybe he did," I admit to him out loud. "But his perfect daughter being found in a place like this would bring the wrong kind of attention. It would play better to his optics if he could say I was kidnapped, missing, or dead."

I mean it to come across as a joke. A morbid one, maybe.

Daze stiffens and releases my wrist. Then he turns away so I can't see his face. "You hate him that much?" he wonders, and I can sense the disgust in his tone. "I've been a pity fuck before, but never a revenge fuck."

I watch the muscles in his back ripple in time with his breathing. Then I prod one with the tip of my thumb and marvel at the firmness. The heat. How he doesn't cringe away from me like he should.

"Don't go hunting," I scold him softly.

"You're right." He grabs my wrist again, evoking a shiver that I feel all the way down to my toes. "I doubt much about you could turn me off, anyway." His eyes flicker down my torso.

"Oh really?" I counter thickly. Any anger my voice might contain vanishes the longer I watch his larger fingers intertwine with mine. "Are you that big and bad? Father could be a mob boss for all you know."

"I *do* know," he says smugly. "Every mobster in the goddamn city, in fact. None of them has a daughter that looks like you."

He could be lying, but a part of me warns he isn't. For a brief moment, I toy with the idea of telling him the truth. Father is Michael Heywood, leader of Covenant and holy savior of the entire city.

"Is that why you stopped me?" I ask him instead. "Because I'm 'not your type'?"

"No..." He lets me go, and his hand falls to the mat with a heavy thud. "I almost killed someone last night."

I feel my entire body tense. Again, he could be lying, but something in his voice makes me doubt that. He sounds so damn tired. Empty.

So, I whisper, "Tell me."

His gaze darts to mine as if he's remembering I'm even here. Then he reaches out, and I inhale as his thumb finds my chin, stroking just below my lower lip. "I mean it. Fuck... I wanted to beat the shit out of him. I wanted him dead."

"Why?" I counter, so soft I barely hear my voice slithering beneath his.

"Because... I could have stopped him," he says without elaborating. "I could have. But then I'd be right back in the fucking thick of it, and I've fought too damn hard to get out the first time. I don't want to be that person again. I can't be..." His gaze darkens as he glares beyond me into some inner universe where I can't follow. "So, I stopped myself. I pulled back. I let him win, but it's like the universe can't let me fucking be a coward for once." He blinks, and when his eyes reopen, he's seeing me again, deploying that unnerving stare. "It's punishing me," he says through gritted teeth. "So, fuck it. I'm done fighting. I'm going to Hell anyway."

"Me too," I find myself blurting out.

He laughs. Then he sighs. "I know what we could do." He sits upright, with his back still to me. He reaches for a pile of crumbled clothing, and I flinch as he tosses a handful of fabric to me. My clothes. "We can get dressed. The gym has a shower—" He nods to a closed door at the back of the room. "Then we can go to my shitty ass apartment and fuck again. Or talk."

He makes both sound equally appealing.

Besides, I'm already at rock bottom, and am too tired to start climbing now.

"Fine."

SEVEN

HE WASN'T LYING. Only a few blocks down from the gym, his apartment lies inside a seedy building that just about fits the definition of "shitty"—especially given the soundtrack of sirens still blaring from another part of the city. Something big must have happened to cause such a racket for so long.

A catastrophe? A major accident? A tendril of fear directed toward Father slips in through the cracks in my psyche. We live near Cherry Lane, in the direction of the city the noise seems to be coming from.

"Hey, space cadet," Daze snaps, intruding into my thoughts. "You coming, or what?"

I turn to find him holding open the door to the apartment building. He lives in one of the housing projects that I always thought resembled a prison, with rusted bars over the windows and paper-thin walls.

"You actually live here?" I wonder, raising my voice as much as I dare. Daze's cocked head warns me that he caught every word.

"What?" He shrugs with feigned nonchalance while leading me up a narrow staircase to the top floor of the building. "You don't like the ambient noise?"

Which currently consists of screaming children and blaring televisions.

I say nothing, and he takes his sweet time fishing a set of keys from his pocket. A second later, he's shouldering open the door, leaving me to enter the apartment on his heels.

"Wow," I find myself blurting with lackluster enthusiasm.

It's cramped enough to feel like a box with just one person, let alone two. A ragged couch sits in the corner, opposite a minuscule kitchen. Empty beer cans litter the floor, mingled with piles of potato chip bags and takeout containers.

What a mess. Ironically, it's the cleanest place I've been in a long time. Home feels soiled these days, filthy with old memories and emotional baggage.

It's not much to brag about.

Though neither is Daze's pathetic excuse for a bedroom—a futon crammed into a space no bigger than a closet. The door to it is propped open with a cinderblock, bringing to mind all sorts of paranoid reasons.

One look at him only cements that thought. His shirt is still gone, allowing his tattoos to catch the light. From this angle, the horseman looks alive, riding the waves of Hell across his back. Literally and figuratively—there's nothing holy about his expression as he faces me directly.

"Last chance to bail," he warns, though there's no real punch to the threat. He sounds more amused than anything. Like he's really issuing a dare. It's only when he raises his hand that I realize what he's holding. Something small and squarish that he sets onto a counter cluttered with dirty plates—a fresh condom. "You have five minutes. Though hell, maybe we could actually *just* chill this time—"

"Or we could stop talking." My fingers fly to the hem of my sweater and catch the wrinkled fabric, winding it up to my ribcage. As the chilled air kisses my bare torso, I feel a fleeting second of something that could be...excitement?

"Come here." He stands like a wall, barricading me from the doorway. With one hand braced against the counter behind him, he leans back and crooks a finger.

My heart stutters at the summons, pulsing like crazy. Odd. I haven't felt this way in forever—something other than...numb. It's like the shock that comes from stepping on a nail. Sharp and unexpected.

"Earth to Frey." I've annoyed him again, letting my attention stray. He makes sure to reclaim it by lunging toward me, jarring me back a step until we're toe to toe, and I'm forced to crane my neck just to meet his gaze directly. Sharp. Honed. Gray. He takes me in with a single, searching flick and then frowns at what he sees.

Like any gatekeeper to desperation, he cashes the check without hesitation—I feel his hand on my thigh now, steadily drifting higher. He unfastens the zipper at the side of my skirt, before dropping to his knees. Working it down my hips, as slow and torturous as ever, he stares up at me with undeniable hunger. Like magic, my thoughts start to scatter like I want them to.

But oblivion comes with a price.

My heart is racing, palms sweating. My skirt now pools at my feet, leaving me in just my panties and a thin, practically see-through undershirt. Daze leans down, pressing his warm lips against my bare thigh as he caresses my legs.

A soft, eager breath escapes me without my permission.

Before long, he stands, and we're locked in a battle of writhing tongues. Harsh breaths. Touching. Touching...

I don't hear the door open until it's too late. When soft footsteps have already crept inside, and a tiny voice utters the words that make us fly apart.

Heart pounding, I spin around, clutching my hands to my chest, but it's a few seconds before I process what I'm seeing. Someone small, ridiculously so, standing in the doorway. A boy? No, a kid. He's barely waist-height, dressed in bright red rain boots and a matching jacket. A mop of blond hair falls messily into his eyes. Eyes so piercing it's like déjà vu staring into them when a twin set belongs to the man behind me.

"Hi, Daddy," the boy says in a deadpan tone as he cuts his gaze to the ceiling. It's almost like he's reading a script, completely unfazed by what he's seeing. "Auntie Lyra says I have to stay with you now," he recites, wringing his pale hands. "Since I'm your *responsibility*." The way he mangles the word proves that he was told to say it, coached by an adult.

Daddy.

Auntie Lyra.

All of those pieces click like a slow-moving jigsaw puzzle.

Then I feel it, that powerful gut punch I've avoided for months since Hale's death. Not even the events of his funeral could make me experience it like this—guilt. Regret. Unbearable self-loathing.

It all descends like a wave, building behind my burning eyes as one question echoes off the inside of my skull—*What have I done?*

EIGHT

"OH SHIT."

The painful reality takes its sweet time setting in, one second after the other. Shame bites into me first. Then guilt. Finally hate. It's the typical symphony of self-loathing I'm more than used to enduring.

As my cheeks heat up to the reddest color possible, I hear something rustling behind me. I turn and barely catch a wad of fabric thrown in my direction—a dish towel, which I assume I'm supposed to use to cover...something. Before I can decide what, I'm shoved aside and backed into a corner by bulldozer strength. Daze.

"Mutt," he stammers, his voice strained. "Hey... What are you doing here, buddy?"

"Auntie Lyra," the little boy repeats on cue. I can't see his face, but I imagine him still staring up at the ceiling, wringing his tiny hands. "She told me that I have to stay here tonight so...so you can learn your *responsibility*—"

"Sammy?" a woman's voice rings out, tense and worried. "Sammy, where are you?"

Footsteps race down the hall seconds after, and another figure enters the apartment. She's tall, with a strawberry-blond head glimpsed beyond Daze's shoulder. My nostrils flare, catching a whiff of crisp, feminine perfume like my mother used to wear. Expensive but simple.

"Oh, Sammy," the woman says sternly. "What did I tell you about holding hands when we—" Her exasperated groan conveys she finally notices the scene taking place in my corner as I scramble to compose myself. "Damn it, Daze! What the hell?"

"What the fuck, Lyra?" Daze hisses, matching her disgust pitch for pitch. "What were you thinking? Bringing him here without telling me—"

"Maybe you should answer your goddamn phone," Lyra snaps. "I was worried sick about you!"

"You have a funny way of showing it," Daze says, laughing in that empty way only he can.

"Have you even been watching the news?" Lyra moves so that I can see her clearly.

If she isn't Daze's sister, she's his clone. Though slightly older, her gray eyes blaze with that same piercing intensity.

"Or have you been too busy fucking—shit. I mean...Sammy, baby?" She switches to a sweeter, softer tone as she crouches before the boy. Smiling for his benefit, she fingers a lock of his golden hair. "Why don't you go into your Daddy's room for a second while we have big grown-up talk time?"

"Wait—" Daze turns and snatches something from the counter. "Here," he says, shoving a bundle of fabric into my arms.

Whatever it is reeks of sweat, and I flex my fingers against the soft cotton, unfolding it cautiously. It's his shirt. Without having to be told, I wrench it on over my head. Thank God it's long enough to cover most of me, including my panties that were on perfect display.

"Well, don't let me interrupt your little party," Lyra snipes from the doorway. Her gaze flicks over me once and narrows.

A white blouse and black slacks only intensify her disapproving mood, reminding me of one of the matrons from primary school. She has the glare down pat.

"Sweetie, you can join the *other* child," she says, gesturing toward Sammy. "Trying out a new breed, eh Daze? At least this one is sober—"

"That's enough. You're my sister. Not my damn mother."

"No," Lyra says tersely. "It's not 'enough.' And yeah, I thought I should bring *your* son to your home, for once. Do you have any idea what a mess you left last night? And then, with everything else going on, I was afraid you'd gone and gotten yourself killed—"

"Jesus Christ, Lyra!" Daze winces, gritting his teeth. "Don't pump my kid with your fucking paranoia!"

"Watch your mouth," Lyra counters. "Though maybe I was worried for the wrong person?" She scoffs and nods toward his hands, which, while clean, display minor bruises. "How the hell are you going to explain *that* to your parole officer? You're lucky Silas isn't pressing charges!"

"*I'm* lucky?" Daze stiffens, his body radiating tension. "Mutt," he snaps to the boy. "Go into my room. I'll be there in a second. And..." He shoots me a wary look from the corner of his eye. "Stay."

"Oh yes, please stay," Lyra says with fake enthusiasm. "Don't let me ruin your fun. Sammy, honey, take Daddy's friend into the bedroom, will you? The adults need to have a little chat."

"Okay." I look down as something warm brushes my hand, and I wind up staring into a pair of eyes so wide they swallow nearly every ounce of light in the room. Endless. "Come on," Sammy says before tugging pointedly on my arm.

Before I can reconcile the consequences, I'm already crowding into the narrow space beside the bed. Without warning, Daze marches over and kicks the cinder block propping the door aside, slamming it shut.

"Just what the fuck were you thinking?" I hear him bellow.

"What was I thinking?" Lyra counters. "What were *you* thinking? Apparently not about Sammy when you beat the shit out of someone on his front doorstep! He is alive, by the way, and conveniently seems to have amnesia, so he hasn't named you. *Yet.*"

"Don't change the subject. You let that fucker into your house," Daze roars. Something heavy slams against the wall. His fist? The sofa? I can't decide which would be strong enough to rattle the apartment to its rafters. "When I let you take custody, you were supposed to, I don't know, *protect* the kid or something? Instead, you serve him up to Silas for 'visitation.' And I'm letting you know now—If I see him again, I'll kill him—"

"Don't even joke. Not with your rap sheet, and I won't be an accomplice next time your ass goes to prison," Lyra warns. "And I can't help that Sammy's *uncle* is a 'fucker' as you put it. Not that fatherhood has taught you much of a lesson. I sure hope you used a condom this time. Maybe you should *think* before you screw someone, eh?"

"So what? You bring Mutt here to punish me? Well, don't you get the wanna-be-mother of the year award?"

"Oh no, you don't." Two sets of footsteps resonate through the floor, heavy and stern. "You listen to me, Daze Marcus Keaton, don't you *ever* insult me like that again. You've been out for what? Three months, and yet you've barely utilized your visitation. Say what you will about Silas, but at least that *fucker* shows up every now and again. Not to mention, he has a goddamn house with actual rooms and clean sheets on the bed for Sam to sleep on, and *he* at least makes sure not to leave beer cans lying around when he does!" Materials rustle, most likely the garbage strewn on the floor. "Seriously, could you at least *pretend* like you want custody? If not for me, then for Sammy's sake?"

"So you can take him back whenever you feel like it? Fuck you, Lyra."

"Fuck me? Well, at least *I'm* on birth control. Look..." She sighs, and I sense lighter steps drifting deeper into the apartment. "Let's cut the bullshit. All I care about is Sammy, and I think that somewhere beneath the booze, you do too—"

"Don't even fuck around," Daze hisses. "You *know* I do."

"Good. Then be here. His school was canceled today because of the mess going on downtown—"

"What mess?" Daze interjects.

"You really haven't been paying attention to the news, have you? Where the hell have you been anyway? I've left you at least a thousand texts... It doesn't matter. There was an explosion over in Cherry Lane. No one's dead. They think it was a gas leak or something, but it's hell with all the traffic redirections—"

"Cherry Lane?" Daze says thickly. "Ain't that where that new-age church is? Salvage or whatever—"

Salvation. The main headquarters is located there, and panic erases everything else like hate and rage. Is Father okay? Was he there during whatever happened?

I look for my cell phone as Daze's voice seeps through the door.

"You said no one was hurt, though? That's good." His voice is a fraction deeper. Louder. Like he knows I'm listening, and that reassurance is directed toward me alone. I'm grateful, if uncomforted in the slightest. "Do they know what caused it?" he adds.

"I don't know," Lyra says. "But since Sam doesn't have school, I can't watch him unless I take off work. Then I remembered that he has a perfectly good father who can do the honors. Let him stay the night. Take him to school in the morning. Be *here* with him. He needs you, Daze."

"I don't need a fucking lecture, Lyra. Least of all from you. How's Jamie, huh? Still a goddamn dropout?"

"Nice one, Day," Lyra says softly. "Shitty mother or not, at least Sammy has someone to tuck him in at night while his dad's out being a goddamn criminal. I mean it, Daze. You blow this visit, and I'll terminate what little rights you have left. Then I'll take Sammy for good, and he'll grow up knowing you only as the delinquent neighbor who sometimes shows up unannounced to family reunions. Do you understand me?"

"Like crystal," Daze snarls. "But tell me one thing? Why tonight, huh? Don't pretend like you don't fucking know what Silas is up to. You doing his dirty work for him now, Lyra?"

"What...what do you mean?" Lyra's voice cracks, betraying unease. "Isn't any night good enough to be with your son?"

"Yeah," Daze admits. "Except the other night you told me to stay the fuck away from you *and* Mutt, and then you pulled that 'permanent custody' bullshit card. So why the change of heart all of a sudden?"

"Don't forget that you begged me to take custody, Day. But... Fine." Her voice lowers, and I have to strain my ears just to follow the rest of the conversation. "You'll find out anyway, but you have to promise me. *Promise* me...that you won't go looking for any trouble."

"That depends," Daze says carefully. "What has that motherfucker done now?"

"Daze..."

"Just say it!"

"Fine! You didn't hear this from me, but...there's a rumor that there will be another fight soon. He's resurrecting the ring, but I don't know where—"

"Looks like your favorite fucker is meddling in gambling again. Remember how you used to ride my dick about 'arms sales'? Now look at what's replaced me."

"It isn't like that," Lyra says quickly. "Besides, *you* stepped down, remember? But I know that you can't seem to resist starting trouble wherever he goes—"

"You're not stupid," Daze says coldly. "Don't pretend like you don't know what a 'fight' means when it comes to Silas. They won't be placing bets on the winner, that's for fucking sure. He's toying with the *mob*, Lyra. With cartels—not the fucking boy scouts! You going to stand aside and watch him start a war, just so long as he lines your pockets? Do you miss the life that fucking much?"

"It's just a *fight*, Day," Lyra insists, but her voice breaks a second time, betraying another lie. "And you don't talk to me about missing the life. You going to get those tattoos removed finally, or what? Besides, Silas promised that nothing would come of it. He has it under control."

"Bullshit! He lied to you. Though what else is new? So much for that fucking uncle of the year award," Daze hisses. "Son of a bitch! I told you to keep him the fuck away, Lyra! You don't watch out and that *uncle,* whose money you love so much? He's going to get Sammy, *and* you killed—"

"I'm not involved," Lyra admits. "Just stay out of it, Daze. Promise me—"

"Get the fuck out."

"Not until you promise that you won't go after him. Think of Sam—he's already lost his mom. You want him to lose his dad too?"

"You want me to watch him? Well, I'm watching him. Now get the fuck out."

"Fine, Day." I hear Lyra move to the door, only to hesitate near what I assume is the threshold. "His bedtime is at eight. He needs to be at preschool by nine-thirty tomorrow, and don't forget he's allergic to tomatoes. And feed him some real food this time, huh? No fast food shit."

"Yeah, yeah."

"Try not to screw up too badly, and I'll let you have him for the weekend, huh? That's what you've been asking for. Just stay in tonight. Please."

The door slams, cutting her off. In the resulting silence, I finally notice faint, persistent scratching noises coming from behind me. I whirl around to find Sammy sitting cross-legged beside an overflowing laundry basket. A red backpack lies beside him, and he has a coloring book on his lap.

"Daddy says I'm not allowed to sit on the bed until he puts on the blue sheets," he explains before I even think to ask.

Currently, the sheets on the mattress are red. Apparently, Daze color codes his rendezvous. Nice to know. God, I can't even look at the mussed piles of cotton, so I stare down at my hands, still shaking, balled into trembling fists. Once again, that resounding question echoes off my skull—*What am I doing?*

I turn just as Daze wrenches open the door to the room. His eyes cut to mine before darting to Sammy. "Hey, buddy," he says softly. "Me and my uh...friend need to chat. Why don't you go find my phone and look up Spongebob? I think it's on the couch somewhere."

"Okay." With meticulous care, Sammy bundles up his crayons and carries his backpack into the other room.

Good. At least he doesn't witness the second I tighten my fist and send it flying toward a face that's the aged version of his.

"Hey! Listen—" Daze snatches my wrist, too strong to resist —tugging my arm as hard as I dare doesn't free it.

"Let me go!"

"Lower your voice," he warns directly against my ear. "I know you're pissed. Okay?"

"Pissed? I'm *beyond* pissed. You have a child?" My voice radiates fury, but it's barely louder than a whisper. "That's typically something you announce before sleeping with someone you just met!"

Isn't it?

"Yeah," he says, nodding. "That *and* the fact that your politician father is planning a run for governor. Or the leader of the free world, or whatever the fuck. Frances *Heywood*. You really thought I didn't recognize you?"

"What?" Shock washes over me like ice water. How stupid I'd been to think I'd found shelter in anonymity. "Get away—" I jerk back only to find myself locked within a vice grip.

"Relax. Frankly, Princess, if I wanted to hurt you, I could have any moment before now."

"But you knew," I croak. "For how long?" A paranoid suspicion sneaks into my thoughts before I can quash it. "Were... were you following me? Did you want to hurt—"

"Don't be crazy," he snaps. "I saved your life, didn't I? But now...I need you to return the favor."

Every muscle in my body stiffens, and I borrow another one of Hale's insults. "Go to Hell."

"Hear me out." He's frowning again, his eyes narrowed and fixated somewhere beyond my head. His teeth seize his lower lip hard enough to draw a tiny bead of blood. With every second, his grip on my arm tightens though he doesn't seem to realize it. "I need you to stay here and watch the kid for a few hours. Two, maybe three tops—"

"Are you serious?" I find myself laughing.

He never does in return.

"Trust me," he insists.

"I'm starting to hate those words—"

"Look, have you stopped to think what might have happened to you if I wasn't there?" He reaches out suddenly and tucks a stray piece of hair behind my ear. The motion doesn't resonate the way it should. I'm not intimidated. My skin heats instead, and I don't pull away. "And I'm not talking about you jumping off some fucking bridge. I know you heard what Lyra said. Your 'church' had a 'gas leak.' You aren't stupid enough to believe that, are you?" He waits, nodding as though my silence is the only answer he needs. "Think why that might be, Frances. It's not like your father doesn't have enemies. In fact, if you knew the full reach of Michael Heywood's influence, your pretty cross alone wouldn't be enough to shield you from his many sins—" He nods to my throat.

And my chest tightens. Too many fears battle for supremacy all at once. *Father. Explosion. Followed.* All I can do is meet his gaze and rasp, "You're scaring me."

He winces as if struck. "Look, I wouldn't ask if it wasn't important. Please. Two—four hours tops. When I get back, I'll explain. About your brother. About my tattoo. Everything I know."

My eyes go wide as I process the implication. "You lied to me—"

"Hale didn't kill himself."

"W-What?"

Daze doesn't even flinch. It's like he transforms in an instant, becoming a colder man with a voice like ice on my skin. I can't even question him. I'm struck dumb.

"He didn't off himself. He was *murdered*," he adds, "and I have a pretty good idea who did it. Do you want to know the truth? Then trust me. Not *them*—your father or your future-boyfriend-arranged-husband, or whatever the fuck—me. Four hours tops."

He lets me go and heads toward Sammy. I watch as Daze lowers to his knee, so he is on his son's level.

"Hey Mutt, Daddy has to go out for a bit. My friend is going to hang out with you while I'm gone, okay?"

Sammy nods, and Daze gives him a quick embrace before standing back up. Witnessing the tender moment between father and son feels wrong. I barely regain my balance before he's already at the front door, wrenching it open. Something makes him look down at his bare chest, and he snatches a gray hoodie from a hook along the wall before storming into the hallway.

"He's allergic to tomatoes. Bedtime is ten, but I'll be back before then."

"Wait!" I race after him, but I don't even catch him descending the steps—he's so fast.

"Four hours," I hear him shout.

And then he's gone.

NINE

I SHOULD CALL the police to report child abandonment. When I finally locate my cell phone, I dial Colton instead, even though he's the last person I want to talk to right now. He's a safer bet than Father, and he'll know what's going on with Salvation.

"Frances?" At the sound of his voice, a wave of guilt and dread descend at full force. "We've been so worried about you! Where have you been—"

"I'm okay," I rasp.

"You don't sound okay," he counters.

He's right. My breathing hitches, my voice broken. "I just needed... A break. Fresh air. I'm fine. What's going on there?"

He says something else I don't catch.

"Frances? Did you hear me?"

"Huh?"

"Your father's been looking all over for you. Tell me where you are, and we can be there in no time—"

"I'm... Okay," I insist. *Not them*, Daze warned. "I just need to be alone for a little while, but I'm safe. I promise I'll check in when I'm ready."

"You heard about the accident, then," Colton surmises. "Is that why you finally called?"

"Yes." I suck in a breath. "What happened?"

"Don't worry, it looks like nothing serious. They think it was a gas leak or something. There was damage to the main building, but thank heavens the work schedule was changed at the last minute. No one was hurt, praise be. It should take only a few days to clean up."

No one was hurt. But the feeling settling in my stomach isn't entirely relief. A last-minute schedule change? I don't remember hearing about it, meaning I would have been there this morning if I hadn't gone to the bridge. A coincidence?

Or fate. I went looking for death when it was already awaiting me.

"You take some time for yourself," Colton says. "I'll help manage your father. I know it's been hard on you since..."

"Colton, I... Thank you."

I hang up, feeling tears break loose. My cheeks overheat with a mixture of shame and frustration. It's like I can feel Hale's disapproval from wherever he may be. I'm disappointing him. Again.

He was murdered.

But how? I saw Hale's body for myself and came to the obvious conclusion. He overdosed. Who could possibly want to hurt him?

Daze could have been lying. But...he had that look in his eye. I can't ignore it. Frustration builds, and I take a page from Daze's book and blurt a word foreign to my vocabulary.

"Fuck!"

"Auntie Lyra says I'm supposed to tell her when Daddy says bad words," a small, disapproving voice cuts in.

Alarmed, I turn to find Sammy standing near the battered couch. A plain cell phone looks massive, held between both of his tiny hands. Despite his warning, his eyes remain on the screen, transfixed by the video playing. "But you aren't Daddy. So maybe I don't have to tell her this once," he insists, flicking his gaze up to mine.

My guess is that "telling Auntie Lyra" is a threat taken seriously.

"I'm sorry," I stammer. "For saying a bad word."

"Okay." Lowering his head, Sammy returns to his show.

Slack-jawed and standing with his little backpack dangling off his shoulder, he's utterly hypnotized. Hale used to tease me when I got like that. Mumbling something about "Kids these days," he'd shut off the TV or video game and drag me outside. Together, we'd hike or play in the garden. Sometimes we'd talk. For hours.

In the end, we'd return home, and Mom would scold us for tracking in mud. When I got older, I realized he had been attempting to do the job she had been too sick to.

He always looked out for me.

"Um...how long does your Auntie Lyra usually let you watch stuff like that?" I ask.

Sammy looks at me in a sheepish way that doesn't need much critical thinking to decipher—*What do you think?*

Not that I have a better way of entertaining him. I turn to the door, hoping that this is all a sick joke and Daze will return. For the first time, the rest of the apartment catches my eye in greater detail.

It's a mess. The longer I look around with a somewhat clearer head, the more my skin crawls. There are more beer cans visible on the floor than there is carpet. An ashtray is in danger of overflowing onto Sammy's little red rain boots. My nostrils wrinkle, catching another scent I instantly recognize. *Weed.*

Hale's room reeked of it.

"Does your Daddy have a broom?" I ask when a full minute passes without the front door opening.

Sammy points toward the fridge, and beside it, I find a mop and a dustpan. Close enough.

Rolling up the sleeves of my borrowed shirt, I enter the kitchen, sidestepping crumpled cigarette butts. On a half-hearted whim, I wrench open the doors to the cabinets under the sink and find a box of trash bags, and some bottles of cleaning fluid. Armed with both, I tackle a heap of garbage, throwing away whatever I can get my hands on.

You're like her when you do that, Hale used to snarl, his eyes bloodshot and unfocused. He wasn't my good, kind, sweet brother in those days. Just a stranger. *What, Frey? You think scrubbing the floor until your hands bleed will wash away the cheating husband or the shitty, fucked-up kids? Think again. You'll learn the hard way, just like she did. We're all just pawns in his game. No amount of cleaning will make him see you.*

Stop. I blink harshly and suck air into my lungs. The stuffy interior of Daze's apartment doesn't help dispel the memory. It just compounds what Hale said in the worst way.

I was never clean. The ache between my legs cements that. Now, I'm just physically broken the way I've always been morally. A sinner through and through.

"Think you can open a window?" I ask Sammy, forcing a smile.

Very slowly, he lowers the phone and climbs on the couch in front of the only window. After a few soft grunts, he exclaims in triumph. "It's open. Can I keep watching Spongebob?"

"Sure." I leave him to it, focusing on the material clutched in my fingers with every descent into the muck.

Old magazines. Chip bags. Beer cans. Beer cans. Beer cans. Daze's trash tells a more cohesive story than he has.

A rustle of plastic alerts me as another can falls into my trash bag from above, delivered by two small hands.

"Aunt Lyra says I'm not allowed to watch Spongebob," Sammy admits. "Please don't tell."

I humor the earnest request with a sigh. "Okay, sure. But...help me clean up?"

Maybe once I can actually see the floor, I'll be able to think. Or at least come up with a logical plan of action. Like call the police on Daze Keaton for child abandonment and go on my merry way. But that would mean forsaking any real answers...

And I'm not ready to face that reality.

Besides, I doubt Sammy would appreciate being shoved into a cop car while the precinct ran an investigation—not that any of this is my problem.

Daze Keaton is not my problem.

Frowning, I tell myself that repeatedly. By the time I've cleared the kitchen, a semblance of concern has eaten at my apathy. How is this man still alive? I'm convinced he lives on a diet of alcohol and nicotine, with the occasional nutrition provided by junk food.

It's like that age-old adage—misery loves company. Daze Keaton must love surrounding himself with empty, broken bottles and crushed plastic. Though, who am I to judge? I've barely lived in my apartment long enough to leave a dent in the mattress, let alone a piece of trash.

Between the two of us, who would win the medal of pity?

I'm not much of a bragger, but Daze, hands down. At least I don't have a kid forced to wipe up my beer stains with a dirty dishrag.

"I'll do that!" I say the moment I spot Sammy on his hands and knees. I take the rag and nod toward the abandoned cell phone. "Why don't you keep watching Spongebob? I won't tell. Promise."

"Really?" His lips part into a smile.

The moment he skips off, I keep cleaning. There's a grim satisfaction in ripping away the harsh, unwelcoming facade of Daze's apartment, revealing the relative plainness underneath. Some tough guy he is.

Without the mounds of garbage, my granny could have lived here, among the simple furniture. Minus the bedroom. Even scrubbed clean and with the bed draped in the "blue sheets," I find shoved in a closet, that room screams bachelor pad, down to the condoms left on the nightstand for anyone to see.

I'm reminded of what Lyra mentioned—*You've been out for three months and barely utilized your custody.*

Judging from the state of the infamous red sheets, it seems like Daze's been too busy working on another round of mouths to feed to focus on the one he already has. What a guy.

A guy I've slept with within an hour of meeting him.

Sighing, I rake my fingers through my hair, contemplating the girl I find watching me from a mirror hanging beside a narrow closet across from the bed.

Weeks without fresh highlights have left my hair scraggly and limp. I look like I'm wilting. My skin is a mess. I'm breaking out all along my chin, and wearing Daze's shirt—and nothing else—I look...

Like the opposite of Good old Frey Heywood. I'm a damned soul of the worst kind—unrepentant when it comes to my corruption.

"Ms. lady?" A small hand tugs on the hem of my shirt, drawing my attention.

Sammy still has Daze's phone in one hand, rubbing his eyes with the other. Only now do I realize how much darker it is in the apartment. The time displayed on the phone's screen proclaims it's just after six. "I'm supposed to eat din-din before my bedtime."

Going off the items in the fridge, his options consist of either beer or week-old milk.

"I...um...do you like pizza?" I wager half-heartedly. It's a never-fail option from my childhood—until I remember Lyra's warning about tomatoes. "Um, never mind. I...uh..."

Think, Frey. I purse my lips, scanning the bare counters and coming up short. In my haste to clean, I think I threw away just about everything that wasn't too big to fit into the trash.

But if Daze truly knew Hale, he'd recognize my brother's trademark phrase.

There is always a plan B.

"Hey, Sammy?" I sink down to my knees so that I'm on his level, able to stare directly into those huge gray eyes. "Do you know if your daddy has any money?"

"Like a piggy bank?" He wrinkles his mouth, thinking. Then he nods and takes my hand, leading me back into the bedroom. Sure enough, underneath a corner of the mattress, we discover a wad of cash tied with a rubber band. How original.

Stealing is wrong. I tell myself that repeatedly as I thumb through the stack of bills. Fifties. Hundreds. There's at least a few thousand right here in my hand.

Any guilt I feel diminishes when I consider how long it's been since he left. Far longer than four hours. It's after six, and Sammy's stomach is growling loud enough to rival the sound from the cell phone. So is mine, for that matter.

"What do you say we go get some groceries for Daddy's house, hmm?" I ask, fighting to sound less malicious than I feel.

"Okay!" Sammy races into the living room and returns with his backpack. Paired with his boots, he looks like a tiny toy soldier ready to embark on an adventure. While I look like his beat-up Barbie doll companion fished from the bottom of a donation toy bin.

"Give me a second."

I slip back into Daze's room and squeeze past the mattress for the closet. He doesn't own much by way of variety. Just a few hoodies, one of which I steal, and some assorted bottoms. Out of the latter selection, only a pair of shorts with a drawstring manages to fit me.

"You ready?"

Sammy nods, and together we tiptoe from the apartment with matching apprehension. The same thought seems to be on both our minds the moment we cross the threshold.

"What if Daddy comes back?" Sammy asks.

I shrug, though I doubt I come off anywhere near as confident as I intend to.

"You have his phone," I point out. And frankly, perhaps a little kidnapping scare is what "Daddy" needs? A fitting consequence for leaving your child with a stranger. "How old are you?"

Sammy wrestles Daze's phone into his backpack. Then he carefully counts four fingers on his left hand and holds them up for me to see. "This much."

"What do you have a taste for?" I ask Sammy while closing the door to the apartment behind us.

Just as we start down the hall, someone calls out, their voice resonating like thunder.

"Where do you think you're going?" A tall figure withdraws from against the wall up ahead, his size imposing. Dark hair shields his face from view, and his black leather jacket and jeans bolster the danger he presents.

I shove Sammy beside me and grapple for the door to Daze's apartment.

"Wait." He steps closer, and a sliver of artificial light falls over his haggard features.

I know him. He's the man from the coffee truck.

"Hi Benny," Sammy says from around my waist. He lifts his tiny hand in a wave.

"Hey, little man," Ben says. "Your daddy asked me to look after you for a little while. I'll be working for the most part, but—" he cuts his gaze to mine. "I'll be parked right outside."

"So, he doesn't need a babysitter after all," I croak. Am I relieved? Annoyed? I can't tell.

For some reason, the image of Daze begging for my help won't leave my brain. The look in his eye...

Fear doesn't fit someone like him. Panic, perhaps. He said that he needed me and seemed to mean it. *Really* mean it.

"This just happens to be on my usual route, and Day asked for a favor," Ben says by way of explanation.

"Good." I shake my head to clear it. "I'll be leaving then."

To go where? Home is out of the question for now, and only God knows the state of Salvation. They might need my help cleaning up, though. And Father might need me...

I start down the hall, heading for the stairs, but Ben grabs my arm before I can even go a step. The second I flinch, he releases me, but he shifts his stance to block my path, making one thing clear before even uttering it out loud, "He told me to look after *both* of you. You're not going anywhere."

"Why?" I demand. "He doesn't own me—"

"He said you might say something like that. So, he wanted me to give you this."

He withdraws a slip of paper from his pocket. A photo, I realize as he hands it to me. The woman smiling in the center of it might as well be a stranger. She's in an industrial kitchen, her blond hair piled loosely on top of her head. This must have been a stealthy snapshot, taken as she was in the middle of serving a tray of steaming dinner rolls.

I recognize this place—the Salvation Soup Kitchen service area.

I remember this day. Six or seven months ago, when I volunteered during the evening meal. That moment sticks out to me for one reason in particular. Hale was there. By then, he'd started avoiding anything and everything related to Salvation. I'd been so shocked to see him.

He stayed for only a few moments, and I caught him leaving out a back door right as we started to carry food into the main dining area. He never said a word to me then. I never knew what made him leave.

Could he have taken this?

An instinctive suspicion makes me turn the picture over, and I gasp loudly at what I find. Writing. Just a few scribbled lines.

Frey.

Five-seven.

Blond. Green Eyes. Always wears a gold cross around her neck.

Hours: 7am—10 am. 6pm—8pm. Weekdays.

DO NOT TALK TO HER—SHE STAYS OUT OF THIS.

That final part had been underlined multiple times in black ink.

Recognition slices through me, and I audibly gasp. I know this handwriting, right down to the lopsided Ts he used to write. Hale's.

"What is this?" I demand, eyeing Ben.

He raises his hands in a gesture of surrender. "I don't know. I'm just the messenger. Daze said he'd explain everything when he got back. Now, why don't you *both* get back inside?" He nods to the door of the apartment. "I'm sure Daze will be back any minute."

"He's been gone all day," I snap. "There's no food in the fridge."

"Really?"

"Unless you count beer as a meal," I add.

Ben frowns. "Fucking, Daze," I hear him hiss under his breath. "What do you need?"

I rattle off an extensive list.

Ben cocks an eyebrow. "You need that fucking much?"

"I'm hungry," Sammy says matter-of-factly. "It's past snack time. Auntie Lyra said to tell her if Daddy forgets my din-din."

"Alright," Ben says. He rakes a hand through his hair and sighs.

"Here." I hand him Daze's money. He could run off with all of it. Frankly, I don't care if he does.

"Stay here," he says before starting for the stairs. "I mean it. If you think I'm bad, you have no idea who might be watching the place from the outside. Stay."

I swallow at the threat. Babysit, Daze said. Why am I starting to feel more like a prisoner instead?

TEN

DAZE DOESN'T COME BACK. Not by seven, when Ben returns to the apartment laden with an obscene amount of groceries. It can't be helped. Compulsive shopping is another one of my bad habits, in addition to cleaning. Hale used to rake me over the coals for it, mocking every outfit I purchased while Mom wasted away.

So much for embodying those selfless tenants of Covenant, Frey.

Sticking out my tongue, I'd counter with a bratty, *Like you do?*

To which Hale would roll his eyes. *Always. I live for nothing if not to serve our father's lofty ideals of perfection.*

It wasn't always a joke. Once upon a time, he meant those words. He wanted nothing more than to live up to our father's expectations. Then, roughly a year ago, something changed. He spoke of our father only with resentment, and the sentiment was mutual.

At least now, I think I've beaten him when it comes to being the family disappointment. I'm still here, wallowing in my trip to rock bottom. Not by choice, however.

After dropping off the food, Ben warned, "I live right down the hall. He'll be back soon."

Apparently, "soon" didn't encompass the couple of hours that passed since then.

Caring for a stranger's son tends to put a lot in perspective, it seems. Eight comes and goes, but when Daze hasn't returned as the clock inches toward nine, I have no choice but to enforce Lyra's arbitrary bedtime. Sammy has a pair of fire-truck-printed pajamas and a toothbrush in his bag, at least. Bundled up in the safe blue sheets, I tuck him into bed.

"You're my daddy's friend?" he asks me.

"Yes," I say, feeling awkward.

"Okay, good night, Ms. Lady. Thank you for din-din." Before I realize it, Sammy's arms encircle my neck in a sweet embrace. It feels so natural to hug him back.

Sammy lays back down and closes his eyes, ready to drift off.

And I could leave. I *should*. My cell phone keeps buzzing with incoming messages, from Colton, Father, and other members of Covenant.

But Hale will never message me again. The closest I can ever come to hearing his voice is running my fingers over the scribbled message on the back of a photo of me. *SHE STAYS OUT OF THIS.*

Out of what?

I doubt Father has the answers. Or Colton.

So... I wait. Long after the hours meld into the early morning. Long after my intuition warns me to call the police for real. When someone finally does shake my shoulder, rousing me awake, I lurch upright, sighing in relief. "It's about time!"

But Daze isn't standing before me.

"I have to go to school," Sammy declares mournfully.

Tears roll down his chin, wetting the collar of his fire-truck top. He's still holding Daze's phone, which is on its last leg of battery life. The time flashes eight-thirty AM and nothing else. Not even a missed call notification.

"I have to be there by zero-nine-three-zero," Sammy insists, his bottom lip trembling. "I *have* to."

"Okay..." I stand and start to pace. Looking around the narrow room, I can tell that Daze hasn't been home. Not once during the night.

Either he's dead or in jail. That's the only way I can rationalize it.

Those two scenarios don't help me much now...and looking at Sammy wringing his pajama shirt in his hands, I don't have the heart to call the police. Yet.

"Do you have your school clothes with you?" I ask.

Sniffling, he nods, and together we find a crisp white shirt and jeans in his backpack, along with clean socks and underwear. Apparently, Lyra didn't judge Daze's parenting skills too highly either because she left explicit instructions taped to the back of the school shirt, including the address.

The doors close at nine-thirty, she wrote. *Nine-thirty! Not a second later, or he'll get a demerit, and it will be on you. Don't fuck this up, Daze! And while I'm on the subject, go over his spelling. Even in preschool, they have pop quizzes, and those fucking prissy teachers think it's odd if a four-year-old can spell DAMN better than BEAUTIFUL. Love you both. Lyra.*

Tossing the note aside, I help Sammy change and feed him breakfast, but he doesn't look any less miserable.

"I need a lunch," he says, his voice hitching. "I don't have my lunchbox. I don't want to eat a 'special lunch.' I don't like bananas."

"It's okay. I'll make you one. Don't worry."

Darting back into the kitchen, I find a Tupperware container in one of the cabinets and set about finding random things to form some semblance of a decent lunch. With a fresh pack of bread, I make a sandwich and rip off the crust—something Mom used to do. A juice box, apple, and a bag of chips form the rest of my attempt.

But it's something.

"There," I say, holding out the container to Sammy, oddly wary of his reaction. "It's a lunch."

He eyes the items with his mouth wrinkled, still sniffling. "Okay."

Now the only other hitch is how to get him across town in twenty minutes. I head for the door and barge into the hall. Sure enough, a voice calls tiredly from two doors down. "Morning, sweet cheeks."

"He needs to get to school," I say, nodding toward Sammy. "Now."

Ben sighs and glances at his wristwatch. "Fucking Daze," he says loudly enough for both Sammy and I to hear. "Come on," he says. "Let's pray the damn thing can even get us that far."

ELEVEN

AS IT TURNS OUT, Sammy goes to school in the same neighborhood I did—something I suspect is Lyra's doing rather than Daze's. I highly doubt a school of this caliber accepts money that's been shoved underneath a bachelor's filthy mattress, that's for sure.

A teacher wearing a gray uniform stands guard near the front doors, overseeing a line of small children streaming into the building. Her eyes home in on our arrival like a hawk's.

"There's Jake," Sammy declares into my ear. "He's my best friend."

The tears are gone, at least. He seems completely oblivious to the attention he draws from every soccer mom in attendance and for all the wrong reasons. For one, he's stepping out of a coffee truck.

Despite it all, his lips form a beaming grin before he races off, tucking a Tupperware lunch under his arm. "Thank you, Ms. Lady," he calls back. "Bye, Benny!"

"You can call me Frey," I mutter, but he's already marching past the teacher, who's too busy staring at me to pay attention to the kids jostling beside her.

Great.

"Come on," Ben says from the truck. "I barely have enough fucking gas to make it back."

"Who said I'm going anywhere with you?"

"Let's not play dumb," Ben snaps. "Daze wants you to wait for him. So, you're waiting for him. Get in."

I'm already inching back, stepping into the main road. One scream would be all it takes to draw attention.

And Ben's wary glance around proves he knows the same thing. "This ain't no fucking hostage situation, lady," he snaps. "Trust me on that."

"Oh?" I scramble back another step, and an oncoming car swerves to miss me. "What else do you call it when some stranger tries to coerce a young woman into his truck?"

He scoffs. "You call it Daze being fucking Daze and dragging me into his goddamn shit. Trust me, sweetheart, you're better off with him than anywhere else right now. Wait—" He breaks off, his head cocked, eyes narrowed. I realize the confusion I gave away just by biting my lower lip as his gaze settles over my face. "You don't know, do you?" He laughs, shaking his head in incredulous disbelief. "I love the bastard like a brother, but Jesus fuck. Even this is too much."

"What are you talking about?" I demand.

Another driver speeds past, cursing at me from their window. One of the school teachers remains standing out in front of the school, staring in our direction.

"I know who you are," Ben says with an exasperated sigh. When I don't budge, he nods to my throat. "I know your holy father likes to make deals with the devil," he adds. "That his little volunteer program—Salvation? Oh, it offers anything *but* that, sweetheart. You think Daze and I are bad news? What about that little bootlicker who follows your father around? Robert something? That guy is the real danger you should be worried about. Trust me, it may look like I'm the one begging you, but it should be the other fucking way around. You need Day, and you have no fucking idea how much."

"He knew my brother," I croak. "Did you? His name was Hale."

"Of course, I fucking knew him. *He* didn't take my advice, however. I suggest you don't make the same mistake." He laughs again, sounding more manic than angry. Turning around, he enters his truck and eyes me from the serving window. "Get in or not. But I wouldn't want to be alone on these streets. Especially if I was you."

He could be lying. A part of me thinks he is. But...

It's his eyes. They gleam smugly. Pityingly, too.

I start forward, ignoring the instinct urging me to run far in the opposite direction. Maybe I will—right after I give Daze a piece of my mind. "Just drive," I say, climbing back inside the truck.

At least Sammy got to school on time. When I finally return to Daze's apartment, I find the door still unlocked.

One thing has changed since I've been gone—a tall figure dominates the narrow space. One look and I'm flying across the living room toward him, teeth bared.

"You jerk!" I form a fist, clenching my fingers so tightly that the knuckles pop.

Surprisingly, I catch him off guard, landing a blow in the center of his chest. He's changed, I realize as my fingers glance off thinner material than the hoodie he left wearing. Now just a thin white T-shirt strains against the muscle shaping his chest. Too thin. It's wet...soaked in places.

With something red.

"Oh my God." I reel back, my head spinning with images that come unbidden.

Hale slumped in an armchair, his eyes unseeing. Vomit-caked pale lips that would never curse me out again. Never say they loved me. Never forgive me.

"Earth to Frey," a harsh voice echoes, cutting through the memories. "Not to be an asshole, but it's a little too goddamn early in the morning for drama. Can you cool it a little? My fucking head is killing me..."

"W-What?" I blink, refocusing on the hulking figure dripping blood all over the floor I spent hours scrubbing clean.

Without an ounce of shame, Daze eyes me boldly through a fringe of matted hair. The red substance is coming from his head, I realize. From this angle, I can't see the exact cause, but that doesn't calm the churning, ominous ache building in my stomach.

"What happened to you?"

He ignores me, glancing around at the corners of the room. "Where's Mutt?"

"Mutt?"

"*Samuel*," he says exasperatedly. "Short little dude with my face. Kind of hard to miss?"

"Sammy," I say dryly. "At least you can *pretend* to care about him."

It's a low blow that lands with more force than my punch. He grunts, his shoulders slumping as a curious expression crosses his face. Maybe it's guilt. His eyes lower to his hands, which look even more bruised in the overcast daylight filtering through the window.

"Yeah, yeah." He grits his teeth and then refocuses his attention on me, his eyes narrowing. "Where the fuck is he—"

"He's at school," I admit. Even I'm not heartless enough to string him on any longer. "Didn't Ben let you know where we were?"

"I didn't have my phone on me." Suddenly Daze deflates and collapses onto the couch, facing me. His legs tremble, betraying just how exhausted he must be. "Seriously, I can't thank you enough—"

"Your head..." My eyes widen at the sight. A long, jagged gash slices across his forehead, dripping fresh blood down his jaw. "What happened to you?"

"Well, Frey," he eyes me up and down as much as he can without lifting his head from the back of the couch and shrugs. "Do you want the short version or the long version?"

"I want the version where you tell me the truth," I say. "You knew Hale, and you lied to me. You knew my schedule. Where I volunteer. What times. Were you stalking me?"

"Don't flatter yourself," he tosses back. "We'll work back from last night's timeline before jumping to any other topics. What happened to me? The *short* version is someone tried to take my head off with a knife—"

"You're lying," I blurt. Nothing in the world should be able to take my focus off Hale—but for a second, he has.

"Alright, you got me." His pained half-smile takes my breath away. "It was more of a machete than a knife."

"Stop playing around!" A series of frustrated steps has me pacing in circles, but nothing loosens the ball of nerves tightening in my chest. He's the only person in the world who affects me like this. I'm no longer numb—just assaulted by senseless, irritating *feelings*. Pain. Confusion. Fear.

I can't stand it!

"Do you think this is all some kind of game?"

"If so, it has pretty shitty odds," Daze admits. "But fine. You want to know what happened? I'll put it in terms a good, church girl like you might understand. About three months ago, I all but sold my soul to keep one of the few people I care about safe. Only, the person I made the deal with? It seems like he isn't happy with my eternal damnation. He keeps fucking with me. Doing little things to piss me off and give him reasons to renege on our agreement."

"Are you saying someone had you beat up?" I add, trying to keep up with his vague metaphors.

"Maybe," he admits. "Though, to be fair, if you think I look bad, you should see the other guy."

"Why would they do that? Hurt you?"

Suddenly, his eyes take on a hard, stern gleam. "Let me ask you something. That outreach program of yours. Have you ever done more than just serve smiles and free food? Do you talk to anyone from there? Really talk? See what happens to them after your family bestows their precious charity?"

I flinch, stung by the vitriol in his tone. "You know what, keep your secrets."

"I wouldn't have left if it wasn't important."

"Important," I parrot, mulling over the word. "Important like making sure you *don't* leave a defenseless four-year-old with a complete stranger?"

"Trust me," he bites out in between more terse grunts. I think he's trying to stand up. When I turn, he has one hand braced against the couch's armrest while clutching his forehead with the other. "That kid is hardwired to call Lyra if so much as a hair falls out of place...but he *didn't*." His voice deepens as he seems to realize that fact for the first time. Gradually, a frown shapes his mouth. "Look, I'm sorry. You didn't have to—"

"And what else was I supposed to do, huh?" I level him with a glare that I hope comes across fittingly harsh. "Leave him alone?"

"Ben would look out for him. But you have a point." Wincing, he leans back against the couch cushions, seemingly overwhelmed, only to groan in pain and bolt upright, rubbing the side of his skull. "Fucking hell."

"You...you're making a mess." My nostrils wrinkle, hating the stench of blood flooding them. "I..."

I barely get the word out as a rush of dizziness leaves me swaying. Watching him conjures up those dark memories again. Images of death I've spent months drowning in a haze. Go figure. The only reason I came here in the first place was to forget, but everything about him just compels me to remember.

"Here—" I turn to the sink and snatch the first object I find. When I approach Daze, he shakes his head, eyeing the dishrag I'm holding with a frown.

"Don't even think about it. I doubt that's very sanitary— hey!"

I cover the cut anyway, pressing hard. "You need stitches," I say in a disapproving tone. "While you're at it, you should get your head examined..."

Warm fingers capture my wrist, making me trail off.

"Thank you." He's staring up at me with one good eye while the one closest to the wound shuts against the pain.

The differences between him and his son are night and day. Sammy didn't have to try to seem earnest, but Daze's irises darken when he attempts anything close... It's disarming. My breaths quicken, and I fight for air.

"I appreciate your help, Frey," he bites out through gritted teeth, oblivious to my reaction. "But frankly, sweetheart, you have the bedside manner of a bull in a china shop. I've got this."

He gingerly wrestles the rag from my grip and dabs at the side of his head a few times before setting the rag onto the floor. Outstretched, his bloodstained fingers feel along the carpet as if searching for something.

"Where the fuck are my smokes? Hey, what the hell?" He eyes the floor as if noticing for the first time that he can actually see it. "Damn. Didn't your mother ever tell you it's rude to mess around with someone else's shit? Where are my smokes?"

"You're welcome," I hiss. "And I threw them out. Every last one."

He stares at me, his bottom lip twitching in horror. "Even the backup stash?" Before I can answer, he digs between the couch cushions and releases a cry of triumph as he pulls out a pack from beneath one of the pillows. "Bingo." He fishes a lighter from his pocket and lights up, inhaling so hard on the cigarette at least an inch of it disappears before he finally breathes out. "Note to the wise," he says through a cloud of smoke. "Always check for the stash."

"You seem proud of yourself." It blows my mind how someone can be so calm. So unfazed despite the world clashing around him—but then it hits me. That's the whole point. He cares about nothing and no one. "How can you live with yourself?" My tone is softer than I intend, almost pitying.

"How?" Daze eyes me from head to toe, exhaling another cloud of smoke. "You're one to talk, sweetheart."

"Yeah," I agree. "But I'm not the one with a kid. I'm not the one who brought a stranger home at random. I'm not a criminal—"

"Yeah, you're just the innocent little *stranger* who fucked me, right? The innocent little virgin who let a criminal pop her cherry."

"Exactly." My cheeks flame, and I grit my teeth against another insult. "And you couldn't even do that right."

His eyes narrow at the insult even as he flashes a devastating grin. "You're a damn liar."

"No," I counter. "You are. So much for that no consequences, worry-free oblivion you promised. Next time, I'll take my chances with the bridge."

"You won't because then you'll never learn why I was really there." He kicks up his feet, lying back sideways across the couch cushions.

"I don't care anymore." If I intended to sound intimidating, I fail. I'm on the verge of tears instead.

"Don't cry." His head is still bleeding, but the fact doesn't seem to bother him. Maybe it's delirium. Or it could be a routine habit—he's been in this situation before.

"Is this a game to you?" I ask, raising an eyebrow. "Dumping your problems on the women you meet? Sorry, but I have my own problems—"

"And I'm sure they're heartbreaking, baby," he interjects, wincing. He cradles his palm against his temple. "Fuck, my head."

"Don't you care about anything but yourself? Your kid, for one?"

"Bingo, sweetheart." He eyes me pointedly and gestures with his free hand as if to say—*Voila.* "You've just answered the million-dollar question. Now you know why I was at the bridge. Not everything has to do with you."

"I'm leaving." I head to the door. My fingers grasp the handle without hesitation, wrenching it so hard the door rattles.

"Wait...I'm sorry."

I push the door open and take a step.

"I...I mean it." A strained note in his voice almost reinforces that fact. Though it could be pain. "I'm sorry."

"And you should be!" I whirl to face him. "You think you know me. You don't know a damn thing!"

My voice breaks on an ugly note—the way it used to when I argued with Hale. When he called me the worst names during our nastiest fight. My chest tightens, restricting the amount of air entering it. *Can't breathe.*

"You think...you think you know, but you don't!"

"Hey!"

My vision blurs, obscuring the figure whose hands land over my shoulders, steering me back against the nearest wall.

"Look at me." He tilts my chin, stroking through the beads of moisture I can't stop from falling down my cheeks. "Breathe. In and out. Nope—" His grip tightens when I try to turn away. "Look at me."

I do, shocked by the concern I find in those watchful eyes.

"Yeah," he murmurs, still stroking through my hair. "...that's it. In and out."

I feel the rise and fall of his chest, goading mine to copy the same steady motion. *In. Out.* It shouldn't be enough to calm me, but it does.

"That's it," he praises as my breathing evens out. I blink, feeling tears spill down my cheeks unbidden, and I realize he's stroking the tangled hair from my face, brushing my forehead with every gentle sweep. "Look at me. Focus on me. I've got you."

"Let me go." I halfheartedly slam my palm against his chest. He doesn't budge.

"No can do, Frey." His voice is harsher than it should be. Guttural. "Hale said you were a spitfire when provoked. No, don't speak yet. Just hear me out—" With every word, his lips nudge my temple. He's crushing me, leaning more of his weight than I can take.

I have no choice but to arch my spine toward him.

Embrace him.

Suffer him.

"Fuck you," I rasp against his shoulder, resigned. Trapped.

"Not today," he tells me with a sigh. "Maybe tomorrow. If you can't tell, babe...I have a pretty damn big headache."

He's still bleeding. I swear I can feel it trickling down my own hairline. Hot. Steady. Salty.

Oh, God. I breathe in through my mouth and try not to picture it. Smell it. Taste it.

"Let me tell you the long version of what happened, free of charge," Daze says, and his voice alone is an anchor against the nausea crawling up my throat. "I'm in deep shit, Frey. Deep, *deep* shit. I...I fucked up, bigger than you can ever know. I thought I could walk away from my old life. That turning over a new leaf would be easy. Boy, was I wrong. I just got way more trouble than I bargained for."

He laughs ruefully, letting the sound trickle against my ear.

"And before you say something smart, it has everything to do with *you*. But you're not stupid. I'm sure that deep down, you already knew that."

Knew what? My paranoid brain plays with a million terrifying possibilities. All those hints I'd tossed his way. *You're a criminal. You're dangerous.*

"Look at me." It churns my stomach how he says it more like a plea than a command.

I can't ignore it, and his height and bulk reinforce how dangerous he truly is. He's right. I've known all along that he wasn't at the bridge on a whim.

"What do you want from me?" he asks.

"The truth."

He looks me in the eye and sighs, teasing me with another hit of his potent breath. I inhale him without meaning to, but this time...I shiver. It's like the nuances of his flavor shift to match the sudden intensity in his gaze. The darkness that paints his irises, deepening the stormy gray.

"Well, I could tell you some fucking dramatic bullshit," he says with a shrug. "Like Frances, your father is a very bad man. He ruined my life. Almost sent me to prison. Had me lose custody of my son—"

"Did you hurt Hale?" I can barely get the words out. It would make sense if he had, and he's been taunting me all this time. He was *murdered...*

"No," he says, and I can't stifle a sigh of relief. "He was one of the few people in this world I owe some loyalty to. A good man. When he wasn't high out of his mind, that is." His quick smile contrasts the gruffness of his voice. "Yeah. I knew him."

I inhale raggedly. "Why didn't you tell me before?" I can't stop the tears from falling, and my hands curl helplessly into fists. I don't know whether to hit him or just...

Cling to his arm and choke down my disgust.

"What he was into... You wouldn't understand. I didn't want to put that shit on you, and he didn't either. He made me swear never to talk to you—"

"That wasn't his choice to make!"

"He wasn't always in his right mind," Daze adds. My chest pangs, and I don't know whether to feel grateful or insulted. He's dancing around voicing one phrase in particular. *"He was unhinged. Crazy."*

Father has no trouble saying as much.

"You didn't know him!" Any anger I might feel dies the longer he holds my gaze.

That look in his eye returns with a vengeance. Fear bites at the back of my mind. I knew Hale was in a rough place—but just how rough was it?

"Tell me."

"He was paranoid," Daze admits. "He came to see me about a hunch he had. It was crazy shit. Conspiracy shit. He thought your father might have been rubbing shoulders with the kind of men who, let's just say, aren't 'holy' in the slightest—"

"Why would he come to you and not the police? Why not

me?" I demand. Hale had issues with Father, but that sounds a step too far.

"The police wouldn't do shit, even if it were true," Daze growls, his hostility apparent. "I didn't believe him at first, but I hate anything involving Michael Heywood, so I played along. I'll be honest, your brother wasn't the sanest crayon in the box, but he was smart as fuck. I'm starting to think he might have gotten some shit right after all."

"Like what?" The suspense is killing me, but Daze seems determined to extend it.

"You have issues against your father. Magnify that times a million, and you'll have a faint idea of how your brother felt. He only wanted to protect you—"

"From you?" I counter, recalling Hale's written message.

He shrugs. "Maybe."

I stiffen, my throat clenching around a hard swallow. "So...*is* this the part where you profess some vendetta and pledge to use me against Father?"

Daze raises an eyebrow—or as much as he can. That simple expression shouldn't be enough to dispel the dread creeping up my throat. It shouldn't.

"Well, fucking you could have been a cheap shot at him—I can admit that." He grimaces—the extent of his apparent guilt. "But it wasn't. I don't care if you believe me or not. And I know I'll sound as crazy as Hale if I try to explain everything to you. I'll show you instead. You have my word on that. Just let me... Get my shit together first."

Grimacing, he gestures to his head.

"So, what do you expect me to do? Sit here patiently while you bleed out?"

He shrugs and fingers a lock of his bloody, matted hair. "Right now? I could use a fucking haircut. But first some painkillers."

TWELVE

"OW! Are you trying to take my goddamn ear off?" Daze jerks out of my reach, scowling at the scissors in my hand. "Go easy on me, baby. I'm already injured. *Easy.*"

"You could always do this yourself," I croak. "I didn't ask for this."

My horror isn't faked. There's blood everywhere. On the floor. On my hands. His shirt is nearly scarlet, and the wadded-up washcloth he has pressed to the wound is already damp.

"You should really get stitches before I cut anymore," I suggest, starting to withdraw.

"No." Shaking his head, he inches back within my reach. "Keep going. I'll live. Don't tell me you're squeamish around blood."

I should tell him exactly that. Still, a rebellious part of me reacts to his tone. "No," I lie.

Warily, I finger a blood-soaked lock of sandy-blond hair before centering it between the scissors' blades and cutting. *Snip.* They join the growing pile of shorn blond locks scattered on the floor.

We're in his tiny bathroom—and I'm baffled as to how the both of us fit in here at the same time. Seated on a rickety plastic chair, Daze faces forward while I trim another piece of his hair.

Nostalgia should be the last thing I feel in this moment. It finds me anyway, and a memory unfurls, one I'd nearly forgotten. I cut Hale's hair once.

We were in his bathroom the night before his acceptance ceremony. He was maybe fifteen... Sixteen. I was twelve or thirteen.

He was so excited to make a good impression and spent hours ironing his clothing and inspecting his appearance.

"Just cut a little at the back," he instructed me, his voice stern.

He wanted to look perfect before the congregation. More than anything, he wanted to impress our father.

"Don't worry about making it too pretty," Daze says gruffly. "I ain't planning on entering a beauty contest."

The memory shatters, and I'm far from the pristine bathroom at Father's home.

"I doubt you could mess up my swag, even if you tried," Daze adds. I think he taunts me merely to claim my attention again. When I meet his stare, he grins triumphantly, and my cheeks flame.

"Oh really?" I turn away and obediently snip another section of hair, but it winds up much shorter than the rest. Serves him right.

He doesn't notice. Instead, he lights up another cigarette and drags on the end like a drowning man gasping for air.

"You done yet?" he finally asks minutes later.

I set aside the scissors and observe him from behind. He's left with a shaggy lob several inches shorter than it was. Grunting, he rakes his fingers through the remaining mane and shrugs.

"Good enough. Thanks."

He goes to stand until I push him back down in his chair. "Not yet," I press, taking his cigarette and putting it out in the grimy sink.

"Dammit, Frey," he snarls.

"You're still bleeding."

"And?"

"*And*, we need to stop it." I sigh impatiently, taking control as I search through the flimsy cabinet for something to stop the bleeding. Superglue. That'll have to do for now.

He turns his head and gazes at the thin tube in my grasp. Yet, he says nothing.

Not a single snarky comment.

That's surely a first.

I attempt to maneuver myself at his side, although there's barely any room for me to get in a position where I can efficiently tend to his wound.

I take over, using the washcloth to wipe away the blood as it trickles down his temple, coating his skin in red. Shifting my weight on my right foot, I lean to the side, trying to find a better angle.

Without the slightest warning, Daze pulls me onto his lap until I'm straddling his waist. My heart leaps at our close proximity.

I didn't know it was possible to feel this way.

Drawing a small breath, I stare straight into his intense, gray orbs. Neither of us looks away. His lips part, and he sizes me up with his eyes. Daring me to be the first to break eye contact...

And I do.

My body begins to tremble as I reach for his face. I can hardly breathe. Hardly think straight.

The room around us spins, throwing me completely off balance.

But he has me. His grip tightens, holding me steady. The warmth of his body sends a shiver down my spine as I force the two flaps of skin back together, coating the gaping wound in glue. He doesn't even flinch. I have no idea what

I'm doing, yet it somehow comes naturally to me, tending to him.

"There," I say, barely any sound to my voice. "All better."

The second I begin to move from his lap, he yanks me back down by my hips, keeping me in place. Our eyes lock. My pulse quickens, stomach tightens, head swims. Overwhelmed, I swallow hard and try to breathe normally.

Nothing seems capable of restoring my sanity. When he reaches for my face with one hand, I can't even move. With unusual gentleness, he cups my cheek against his palm. He holds it there for a second, maybe longer. Time grinds to a halt as he leans forward and his lips crash against mine.

Instantly, the whole world falls away.

I lean into him, boneless. Unrestricted, he deepens the kiss, tilting his head to the side, and slips his tongue into my mouth. Joined like this, we move in sync, breathing heavy. The scent of copper and musk overwhelms my system.

He ignites a burning frenzy of confusion and passion deep within my soul.

This is wrong.

This is so wrong.

But, God, then why does it feel so *right*?

As if to drive that point home, I feel his hands trail down my back until he cups my ass, clutching me to him.

"Your innocence drives me fucking wild," he breathes into our kiss, slipping his fingertips beneath the waistband of my shorts.

The heat from his palms feels like fire against my skin. My pulse accelerates. No man has ever touched me like this. Felt like this. A foreign sensation takes over my body, making my hips arch to chase it, until he slips further back. Lower. *Lower*.

Reaching behind me, I grasp his wrist.

He stiffens at the contact. In one swift motion, he stands, easing me onto the sink. His hands fumble with my shorts and panties as he tugs them down my legs, leaving me bare. Rather than recoil at the act, I fist his hair, kissing him harder, drawing him closer.

"Damn." He groans deeply against my lips. "I need to taste you, Frey."

"You already have."

"No." He bends down and brushes his lips against my inner thigh. "I need to *taste* you. Every part of you," he clarifies.

I don't understand. Not until his calloused palm graces the space behind my knee, urging my legs further apart. Ablaze with a hunger I can't name, he stares...

There. My cheeks catch fire, and I try to clamp my knees shut. "Very funny—"

"You are so beautiful." The awe in his voice shocks me into going limp, and he easily bares that part of me to him again.

Beautiful. I'd spent my whole life believing this part of my body was linked to dangerous temptation. That, out of desire for it, men would be reduced to mere animals, eager to hurt me. Use me.

None of those characterizations fit Daze. When he sinks into a crouch before me, I don't resist. Not even when his fingers caress me in an intimate way that makes my eyelids flutter.

Then a newer, strong sensation overrides his touch, and my back bows. Unconcerned by my wide-eyed stare, he takes me into his mouth, and every part of me spontaneously tenses. My mouth falls agape, and a hushed moan escapes me. The sound only seems to encourage him. He licks, sucks, and nibbles my most sensitive flesh, working magic with his tongue.

I gasp.

He groans, savoring the taste of me. Relishing in the way my hands find his head, tugging hard on his hair. Sinking one finger inside me, he flattens his tongue over a bundle of nerves near my center, and it's electric.

I whimper, giving in to the new sensations of this beautiful attack on my body.

"Good girl," he lets out, his warm breath caressing my skin. "Fuck," he purrs, working in another finger, stretching me wide. I fight through the soreness. His pleasured, throaty grunts of approval make it all worth it. "You're so goddamn tight."

"Please," I gasp, breathing fast. Shallow. "Too much—"

"I know," he says, his voice guttural. "I need you to come for me, Frey. Come all over my face," he commands, his voice like silk. He flicks his tongue over me, again and again, and thrusts deeper, curling his fingers, finding just the right spot.

Wetness pools between my thighs, trickling down onto the cold surface of the sink beneath me. I writhe against his face, letting out helpless little cries.

And he groans his approval into me, heightening the overwhelming pleasure. "That's it. Good girl," he bites out, finding the perfect rhythm with his tongue and fingers.

And I come undone, spiraling.

Spiraling. *Spiraling*.

"Fuck, baby. Is that the spot?" He sharply exhales, pumping his fingers into me faster. My breathing quickens, toes curl, thighs tighten around his neck. I convulse against him, and my loud whimpers echo throughout the small space around us as he devours me with his mouth.

It's too much to bear. I try to squirm away, but he slips his hands beneath my thighs and pulls me back to him.

"Daze," I gasp, gripping the edge of the sink so hard my knuckles turn white. "Oh, God—"

He stands without warning, leaving me a hot, desperate mess. Reaching behind me, he retrieves a condom from the cabinet. He slips it on, and without wasting any time, he's inside me.

"Fuck," he bites out.

He firmly grips the back of my neck and locks me in place, pressing his forehead to mine. Thrusting deep. *Deeper.* Nearly splitting me in half. I breathe through the discomfort and pain until my body adjusts to him. When I do, he moves faster, inching me further up the sink with each forceful thrust. Again. Again.

Slower. Deeper. Harder.

Desperate, I brace on his broad shoulders, holding onto him for dear life.

We finish together, holding each other's gaze, breathing unevenly.

Before I can make sense of it, he pulls out of me and steps to the side. Reaching past me, he turns on the faucet and wets a washcloth with warm water. Gently he places it between my thighs.

I'm immediately caught off guard by such a kind gesture. Enthralled, I study his face as he cleans me gently. Maybe I'm not just an afterthought to him...

And there *was* a spark between us. That deep-seated impulse made writhing against him in a tiny bathroom seem...sane. Logical. It was more than mindless lust.

He tosses the washcloth into the tub before locking his eyes with mine. We share a heated, intimate stare that leaves my heart fluttering.

"Thank you," I whisper.

His face softens, and he nods before tossing the used condom into the trash. Stepping back, he fixes himself in his jeans while I hop down from the sink and step back into his shorts and my panties.

"Frey," he blurts out, stepping closer. He's limping, leaning heavily to one side. There's an ache in his voice, rasping beneath every word he speaks. "There's just something about you. You're... so different."

"Different?" I echo softly.

"You make me feel...things."

"Is that a bad thing?" I ask.

"No," he nearly whispers, brushing a loose strand of hair behind my ear. "Well—fuck. Maybe. I'm not so sure."

He lights up another cigarette as he looks into the mirror, examining his head. My thoughts begin to race as I tie the string of his shorts tighter around my waist. I still have so many unanswered questions.

"Daze," I begin. "I just want one thing from you. Please. Just tell me the truth."

He cracks a smile that could almost pass for genuine if he weren't wincing. "Do you really want to do this now?"

"Yes," I press. "Tell me what you know about Hale. Why do you have this picture of me?"

I brandish it, but he shakes his head, sending more stray bits of cut hair to the floor. My eyes latch onto the mess as a familiar itch nibbles at my nerves. Before I know it, the photo is in my pocket again, his mop is in my hands, and I'm using it to gather his hair into piles.

Neat. Orderly. Giving into those impulses is the only semblance of control I can grasp—especially after what just happened with Daze. For the time being, I push the sordid scene to the back of my mind and try to recall my old methods for regaining calm. Pray. Obey. Be patient. I was taught never to disobey a rule or law or to be a slave to vice. It's funny how things can change seemingly overnight.

The strangest part is that I don't feel as lost as I did on the bridge. I'm just tired.

"Let's try something different, huh?" Watching me, Daze leans back, propping his elbows against the nearest counter, and the neglected cigarette spills loose ash against the floor.

"What game do you want to play now?"

"No game," he says softly. "Just the brutal honesty you've been dying for."

"Why did you lie?"

Satisfied by my response, he nods and inhales his cigarette so hard the end glows red. "That's it," he murmurs, exhaling in a long, slow line. "I lied because I didn't think you could handle the truth."

I swallow hard. "And now?"

His eyes narrow. "I've dicked you around long enough, Frey," he admits bleakly. "You can take it. Hell, if you want the truth, you're gonna have to."

"You're right." Straightening my posture, I cross my arms. "I *can* handle it."

"You want to learn what Hale was up to? Then do me a favor. Come with me. As I said, it's better if you see for yourself, and I might as well kill two birds with one stone while we're at it."

"Kill?" I echo.

"Yes." He chuckles, but the sound comes out colder than ever. "*Figuratively*, Frey. Don't take this personally, but you're just about the only person I can trust right now. Don't you feel special?"

"Are you serious?" I eye him skeptically, alarmed when he doesn't crack that playful grin.

"Damn right," he says. "Do this for me, and you run back to your perfect life having tasted the dark side, and I get to do my good Samaritan deed for the day."

"No," I insist, squaring my chin. "You said Hale was murdered—"

"We'll get to that," he says harshly. "Your brother had to learn this lesson, and so will you."

"Fine," I concede, exasperated. "What's the favor?"

"Be with me tonight." When I flinch, he shakes his head. "No, not like that. I mean... I need someone I can count on to get me out of there without...distractions."

I shiver at his tone. Gone is the cocky arrogance. He's worried. "What kind of place is this?"

"Hell," he grates. "I need someone there to remind me of that, every fucking second. It's a good thing your family bathes in fucking holy water. If there was ever some small shred of good in me..." He sighs and fixes me with a probing stare. Slowly, he nods. "You'll draw it out, I think. You'll make me stop. Don't worry. This shouldn't take long."

"Is this place...legal?"

Daze smiles in that disarming way, making the air catch in my chest. "Baby, nothing I do is legal."

I'm thrown off when he turns away, hiding his expression from me. His shoulders stiffen, suddenly rigid.

"And what are we going to do while we're there, exactly?"

"We've got to plant some bait," he answers, meeting my gaze directly. "You want to know about your brother, right? What *really* happened to him? Well, I'm going to take you somewhere so you can get your answers. But first, I have to provoke this bastard into inviting us. You'll see, Blondie. Just keep those eyes open."

"Okay."

"Good. Do this, and you got me, however you want me. I'll owe you big. After tonight, you can put a leash on me, baby, and walk me around the whole damn city. Just don't make me say please."

If he's joking, it's too cruel to even acknowledge. But if he's not...

I have no other way of finding the truth.

I owe Hale that much.

We don't leave right away. After insisting on another cat nap, Daze finally seems ready to move. Almost, anyway. "Five minutes, Frey," he prods before dragging me into his bedroom. "We've gotta make a fashionable entrance."

He must mean the opposite, considering that what he hands me next is a skimpy dress with a plunging neckline wrenched from the back of his closet. The black fabric smells faintly of perfume but isn't wrinkled, presumably clean. There are no tags on it, however. Whoever owns it left it here for Daze to loan out to any stranger he happened to bring home.

"This belong to another woman you talked off a bridge?" I croak, fingering the spaghetti straps. I follow as he enters the bathroom.

"Something like that. Put it on. And this—" He shoves something else into my hand, and I gape at it—a shiny, fire-engine red wig. "Hurry up. We need to leave soon."

He's gone before I can choke out another question, closing the door behind him. Left with no other option, I shimmy out of his shorts and tug the dress on over my head.

"Don't forget the wig," he calls through the door. "I can't risk anyone recognizing you, Princess. No one will fuck with you if they think you're with me, but you gotta look the fucking part, and blonds aren't my type. You done yet?"

I jump as the door is shoved open, forcing me to scramble out of its path. Crossing his arms, Daze inspects me, frowning. "Good enough. Here—" He enters the bathroom and rummages beneath the sink. Eventually, he surfaces with a small black case he shoves onto the counter. Through a clear lid, I can make out a simple selection of dark eyeshadow.

"What am I supposed to do with that?" I wonder helplessly.

"You know." He mimes applying makeup. "Get dolled up. The cakier, the better. Prissy little politician's daughters aren't welcome where we're going, and I'd bet my ass you won't find another fucking *Frances* there either. Now make yourself look like a Rhonda or a Candy."

"So, basically a stripper?" I eye myself in the mirror again.

As sheltered as I've been, I shouldn't have a reference in mind —but I do. It's a fleeting memory of one night Hale, and I crept to the top of the stairs and watched my mother storm out of the house. She wore heels taller than I was, her eyes caked in a dark substance. It was like she transformed, becoming someone apart from Abagail Heywood, the reserved Shepherd's wife.

She looked like a demon.

And, a voice in my head whispers, *you're following right in her footsteps.*

"Yeah, a stripper." Suddenly, the makeup case is snatched from my hands, and my chin is in Daze's grip. "Hold still." Grunting, he flips open the case and runs his thumb over an ugly shade of navy. "Stop blinking!"

"Okay! Okay!" I suffer his clumsy application and nearly gag when I look at myself in the mirror. I don't look like my mother. With the blue eyeshadow and terrible wig, there is no resemblance to me at all. I'm a stranger.

"Perfect," Daze says in approval. "Now, one last thing..."

"W-What are you doing?"

I shiver as his hand grazes my waist, snagging the hem of my dress. Before I can shove him off, he lifts, revealing my panties. Then my stomach.

I stiffen. He can't possibly intend another repeat of what happened earlier. Can he? I don't know. His body visibly tenses, muscles twitching, as he takes in the sight of me.

And, despite my better judgment, my breathing hitches. Those crippling doubts disappear. I feel that spark again, and chasing it doesn't feel half as stupid as it should. "D-Daze—"

"Frey," he murmurs, briefly lifting his head to look me in the eyes.

My heart hammers as my lips dampen and part. "I—"

"Keep this on you at all times," he warns, tucking something between my hip and the waistband. It's cold. Heavy...

As I look down, my stomach sinks. Not only are his fashion choices questionable, but Daze has a weird idea of an accessory for this outfit—a small utility knife.

THIRTEEN

JUST OVER TWENTY-FOUR hours after Daze stopped me from jumping, and everything I suppressed comes rushing back. I miss the quiet, sterile walls of Salvation. I miss Father's stern words of encouragement and his aversion to cursing.

I miss the numbness of missing Hale but never knowing why he might have hurt himself. I thought answers would bring me clarity, but it's been the opposite.

I've only found more questions, and I'm not sure I want them explained.

"Let's get this shit over with," the man beside me hisses. I shoot him a wary glance. An unfamiliar note has crept into his voice. It makes him sound harsher. Meaner. Like...

Well, like the criminal poster child he appears to be. He seems committed to the role—like any "bad boy" cliché, he even owns a motorcycle. It sits outside in the alley just beyond the gym. I don't have much experience with such machines, but his is matte black, with white and silver details painted on the body—a fitting ride for a man who thrives in sin.

"Oh, don't look at me like that, Princess," he scoffs, noticing my raised eyebrow and the hands placed on my hips. "This baby rides like a dream. Even in *that* outfit, you don't compare."

To counter him, someone whistles nearby, and I cross my arms, suddenly self-conscious. Dressed like this, standing on a street corner could unintentionally ask for a whole world of trouble.

Much like the man already wreaking chaos in my life. He *breathes* trouble.

And yet, I can't stop inhaling whatever poison he chooses to exhale.

"You ever ride before?" he wonders from over his shoulder.

I shudder with apprehension—and not entirely because of the prospect of riding on the back of a dangerous vehicle. In the waning daylight, the cut on his head looks even worse. He didn't bother to change from his ratty clothes, and together we make quite the picture. He found a pair of heels in his mystery box of women's clothing to go along with my dress and wig. Balancing on stilettos was never my forte, sober or otherwise. I can't even imagine what Nanna might think to see me now.

She'd go to Covenant and pray.

"Earth, to the princess." Daze snaps his fingers before my nose.

"Of course not," I say, sensing that he already knew as much.

Rather than issue a taunt, he tosses me a helmet that had been previously dangling from one of the bike's handles. "Here."

He comes up behind me as I wrestle it on over my wig. "You wanna do this in the front or the back?" he murmurs, his breath hot on my neck. "Though, something tells me you don't enjoy doing *anything* from behind."

My cheeks flame at the memory of the stunt he pulled in the bathroom. I'm unsure what extent he would have gone to if I didn't stop him. "Enough joking," I snap. Ducking out of his reach, I straddle the edge of the seat unassisted. "Just drive, or whatever you do with this thing."

"As you wish." Laughing, he mounts the bike from the front. Then he reaches for my hand, coaxing my fingers to palm his stomach, alarmingly close to his pelvis. "Just make sure you hold on tight."

I'm blushing, but he doesn't seem to notice or care. *Vrrrom!* The next second, the bike roars to life beneath us, and there's no choice but to wrap my arms around his waist or fall off.

"Hold on," I hear him warn above the grinding growl of the engine.

Gritting my teeth, I reposition my hands, squeezing him even harder. An unsettling realization creeps in as my body seems to relax into him against my will. Fire sizzles beneath my skin, but it doesn't feel painful—the way I suspect hellfire should. My life has been one sermon after the other on the perils of sin, but the truth is... I can't deny the feeling his nearness alone gives me. *He* gives me.

A wild, thrilling, electric feeling.

Maybe he's my punishment, created solely to tempt me to sin...

And to make me relish every act of corruption on my way down to Hell.

Our current surroundings reinforce that comparison—this part of Westpoint City is a perfect allegory for Hell. Father always warned me against venturing to the "bad side of town." Even as a child, the irony wasn't lost on me. He praised the downtrodden parts of the city and touted his work with the less fortunate. Hale and I volunteered for his charity, meeting people from all walks of life.

But in private, he referred to those same areas as slums filled with criminals and deadbeats who might corrupt my poor, innocent soul.

They call it the wrong side of the tracks for a reason, Frances. Once you're there, there's only one way to get back—but it's not so easy if a train is coming.

He was right—only Hale's death was that train, and contrary to Father's belief, I'm not looking back.

I'd probably fall off the bike if I did.

Reckless speed makes for a heart-stopping trip through the city at the height of rush-hour traffic. Without care for safety, or something mundane like laws, Daze weaves in and out of lanes like Hale would when playing one of his stupid video games.

Without fear of death.

"Think you can slow down?" I practically scream into his neck as a bus careens dangerously close to our path.

If he hears me, he doesn't react. Instead, he cuts across four lanes to make a right turn. *Thunk!* The engine cuts off a second later, throwing me against him.

"Easy, baby," I hear him grunt as he stabilizes the bike near a rack containing at least five other motorcycles. "Don't wreck the merchandise."

The flat of his palm lands over my thigh, and I just stare at it. I'll never get over how lethal a collection of muscle and bone can seem when shaped into hands like his—and yet how gentle they can feel on me. In me...

"Earth to Frey," Daze warns.

Startled, I scoot back and nearly fall. Only by steadying one of my ridiculous heels against the ground can I maintain my balance.

"Now look..." Daze stands, shaking out his newly-cut hair. His eyes draw my attention, darker than they were before we left. His posture is tenser too, and he doesn't look at me directly, even as I yank off his helmet and dump it on the seat of the bike. "The world in there isn't like your little church."

He jerks his chin to a brick building about a block down. It looks like a warehouse at first glance, but there's no sign or display to give any clue as to what lies within.

"The men inside might not be as polite as your parishioners," he adds, eyeing his knuckles. "Do some shit that may turn your delicate little stomach. Think you can handle that?"

This time, the jokes don't have that biting sense of humor tainting them. His eyes don't sparkle. His mouth holds that serious, firm line that makes the tiny hairs on the back of my neck stand up.

He's serious.

"And you've been *such* a gentleman so far," I choke out.

"I have, haven't I?" He flashes a real grin. His eyes rove downward, and his tongue traces his lower lip in a slow, disconcerting motion. I suck in a breath. It's like he knew where my thoughts had drifted seconds prior.

And they eagerly head there again. I can't help it. His eyes do something strange when his attention turns to that vulgar, taboo subject. Sex. It makes it harder to breathe—impossible to think of anything else.

He distracts me so much that the rest of the world has to fight for my attention. A honking horn does the trick, and I turn to the road. Even on this back street, traffic runs at a steady pace, and a passing yellow school bus draws my attention.

"Sammy," I blurt. "Don't you have to pick him up from school?"

"Lyra's got it." His palm graces the seat of his bike as if saying goodbye to the thing, then he turns and heads up the street, leaving me to follow.

"You're not even going to call her and check?" Poor Sammy. I picture his face, streaked with tears, as he stares at an empty school parking lot. "Shouldn't you—"

"I *know*," Daze insists, waving me off. "She's got him. That's the game she plays. She'll let me get a fucking taste, then hold him hostage for a week. No contact. No picking him up from school. Nothing. The next time she wants something, she'll dangle visitation again. Rinse and fucking repeat."

The muscles in his arms quiver with tension—a brief crack in his carefree facade. I've written him off as a selfish deadbeat. Maybe I still should. But...

There's more there. He's so much like Hale the comparison stings—they both enjoy keeping secrets from me.

And they both have a way of getting under my skin.

"Knowing that, you sure spent a lot of time with him," I counter. I know what it's like to have absentee parents. "Don't you think—"

"Don't." Daze stops so suddenly I stagger against his back. "Don't act like you know how the fuck I feel about my own damn kid because you don't. I'd die for him. Hell, as things stand now, I might as well be dead. He'd be better off."

The coldness in his tone chills the air in my lungs. I can't find anything to say. Then, I manage to croak out something. "I'm sorry."

"We don't talk about *your* shit, and you don't talk about mine. Got it?" He looks back to see me nod once. "Good. Let's go."

We continue in silence and quickly draw near the warehouse. Up close, I'm caught off guard by how unassuming it looks. There are no lights in the dusty windows. No noise drifting from beyond the walls. No sign proclaiming "Debauchery Within." Rather than approach the metal doors I assume serve as the entrance, Daze cuts through an alley and side-steps a dumpster overflowing with trash. There's another door on this end. When he raps on it with a fist, it opens from inside.

"Oh fuck. Not you." A man wearing a leather jacket and jeans bars the doorway. He eyes me up and down before turning his attention to Daze, who suddenly lingers in my wake. Baring his teeth, he spits on the pavement. Is this the man we've come here to provoke? "You again?"

"Me again?"

I turn. That voice *sounded* familiar. Daze—only about two octaves deeper than he usually speaks. Standing tall, he meets the man's gaze without flinching. They eye each other for a second. Two. Sighing, the stranger finally steps aside.

"Chris can't protect you this time. I bet my ass that Silas will show up in less than five minutes. You should clear out, Day. Most of us have no beef with you, but... Rules are rules, and you're *persona non grata* after that stunt you pulled."

"Thanks for the warm welcome," Daze replies coldly. "Now, let us in."

For a second, it looks like the man won't budge. Then he shrugs. "It's your funeral. Don't say I didn't warn you."

"I won't." Daze grabs my wrist, steering me inside ahead of him. It's dark and dank. My nostrils itch with a moldy stench that reminds me of how the city sometimes smells when it rains. Damp, drenched dreams mixed with the faintest hint of cigarette smoke.

"Watch your step." Daze reaches past me, opening what I assume is a door. Just like at his gym, his hand finds my hip next to guide me down. A part of me latches onto the contact. It means it was an act, right? He isn't that cold, hard person I just caught a glimpse of.

Not entirely.

As we descend, orange light floods in, revealing a wide, spacious room. There's a bar at one end, lined with stools. Across from it are a few pool tables. It's not the den of vice I pictured.

"What is this place—"

"Not yet," Daze warns.

The back of my neck prickles, picking up on his unease. He's as edgy as he was the day he led me across town to his gym. As if any minute he expects an attack. As a result, he's closer, running his lips along my neck. The touch doesn't convey the same electric tension I felt in the bathroom. In this instance, he reminds me of a dog, guarding his favorite bone while surrounded by potential rivals. He's possessive of me, and it feels strange to acknowledge that.

But it shouldn't feel...good.

"Don't worry," he says near my ear. "This isn't the hard part. We've got to plant a little bait first."

"What?" I crane my neck to look back, but his expression reveals nothing when it comes to his motive. Bait?

Confused, I put my focus into scanning our surroundings. With every new observation, a ball of dread in my belly grows tighter. Painful. I try to picture Hale here, mingling with these hostile people. Breathing in air tinged with cigarette smoke and deafening music.

I can't quite envision it. No matter how bitter and angry he became, he'd never fit in here. Not like Daze does, bulldozing his way fearlessly through the crowd.

I'm tempted to break his rule by asking a question. "Why are we—"

"Keep close and stay quiet," he hisses, his eyes fixed ahead. "I'll do the talking."

The order alone isn't what makes my mouth snap shut—it's his tone, conveying an authority he didn't even utilize around his own son. Intrigued, I follow his gaze to a man leaning on a pool cue against the back wall. His black leather jacket seems out of place in the casual surroundings, as does his harsh smile.

"Daze," he calls over the music. "For the love of God, you got a death wish? You could use a gun, you know?" He mimes one with his free hand and pulls the pretend trigger, aiming his forefinger at his skull. "It's quicker and would make a hell of a lot less mess than having to peel you off my goddamn floors every night."

"And what, Chris?" Daze asks, lifting his arms into the air. "Spare you bitches the fucking show? No way."

"You always were insane, even before you went away." Chris scoffs and aims his cue at a row of balls neatly lined on the pool table. He strikes, sending them in every which direction. "Not that I used to complain. It made you a damn good leader. But now?" He looks up, meeting Daze's gaze, and laughs at what he finds. "You're even more fucked up now than you were then. Usually, power is what corrupts most men. Not 'freedom.' Though, you always did have a way of making a mess, even when you were on the straight and narrow."

"What can I say? I'm a man of many talents," Daze quips with a maniacal smile—but his voice still has that sharp edge to it, and the amusement doesn't quite reach his eyes. "Once I have a nice little chat with Silas, I bet you won't see me around here for a long, long time."

"Silas." Chris narrows his eyes and places the bumper of his cue stick against the floor. "When I heard you were back in town, I was stupid enough to hope you had changed your mind."

"What?" Daze says, raising an eyebrow. "You mean to say you all aren't better off without me, frolicking in the sunshine?"

Chris doesn't crack a smile in return. "No. We aren't. Don't pretend like you haven't heard the rumors. About who Silas has been working for, dragging the Saints into his mess. I'm sure that's why you're really here, but you'd be a fool to go against him alone. The kind of men pulling his strings have more power than you can imagine and enough wealth to make even the police look the other way. Though, if you were looking to get back into the fold... That could change things."

"I don't know what you're talking about," Daze says, matching his serious expression. "I'm just passing through."

"You're playing with fire, Day," Chris says, an eyebrow slightly raised. "You were always a reckless punk, but suicidal? I never took you as such."

I can't escape the suspicion that the majority of their conversation is transpiring beyond their words. It's all in the steady way Chris maintains their eye contact for only a few seconds before turning away, a frown tugging at his mouth.

"Coming here tonight was a mistake," he reiterates. "You may have stepped down, but he's not going to stop until you're dead, you know," he mutters, crossing his arms. I notice the same patch on his jacket sleeve that Ben wears—the skull with wings. "That son of a bitch can't let it go. You gave up everything, and he *still* isn't satisfi—"

"Let's not get sappy, Chris. Besides, if I'm going to die tonight, I'll need a drink. Or several. And one for my friend." He slams his hand on my shoulder, nearly knocking me over. "But make hers a virgin. She's a sloppy drunk."

I don't know whether to be insulted or relieved by the request. I've never sipped anything other than the wine served at Covenant events as part of the holy service.

"If you say so." Chris gives me a final once over before crossing to the bar and grabbing three glasses from behind the counter. He slams them onto the surface and fills two with brown liquid from a glass bottle. The last one he tops off with water. "For the lady," he says, sliding the glass toward me.

"And for the men." Daze grabs both glasses and clinks them together. Then he downs both, one after the other, wincing at the taste. "Fuck, that shit is strong, Chris." He coughs, slamming a fist against his chest. "You trying to finish me off, yourself?"

Laughing, Chris retreats to the other side of the bar. "Silas would pay me handsomely if I did," he calls back. "Watch yourself, Day. I'm sure he's already on his way."

Instantly, Daze's smile falls, and he tilts his chin toward me. "It's only a matter of time. Just follow my lead and trust me. Please."

I stiffen at his unease. "What are you talking about?"

I look over at Chris, but he's out of view, presumably having gone into a back room.

"I'm talking about answers, Frey. You want to know what Hale was looking into? Well, the Saints are part of it. I'm sure you figured that out, though."

Because he'd lied about Hale's drawing meaning nothing to him. It was a clue. But why would my brother be interested in what seems to be a criminal outfit?

"Look—" Daze shoves both empty glasses across the counter, but he's even stiffer now. Anticipation radiates from him in steady, unsettling waves. He's waiting for something, but the caution doesn't seem directed at Chris.

Perhaps at this unspoken figure who supposedly will be lured out by our mere presence.

"This could take a while. In the meantime, ask me what you want. I'll do my best to answer it. First, play along. Lean in but don't make it obvious."

He taps his throat with a finger in a silent command. Nervously, I lean forward and press my lips right by his pulse point. In the back of my mind, I understand his reasoning— to anyone watching, it must look like a playful kiss—not a stomach-churning moment before I finally get the answers I've been craving.

Impatient, I start with what should be a simple mystery for him to solve, "How did you know Hale?" I murmur against his skin. In spite of everything, his taste worms onto my tongue—musk and sweat. It isn't revolting, though, and I don't clamp my lips in disgust. My tongue dampens instead. Good Lord, no one on earth should taste so good.

"He came looking for me," he mutters back. "I don't know how he found my name, but he offered me cash to help him out."

My eyes widen. "Help him with what?"

"A little mystery he wanted to solve," he says cryptically. "He needed my expertise to navigate a rougher part of town compared to where your fancy church is. In the end, I think he found way more than he bargained for."

It's an ominous statement, but it's also too vague—like there's more he hasn't said. "What aren't you telling me?"

With a sigh, he shifts to face me and fingers part of my wig, playing with the synthetic strands. Finally, he inclines his head. "What do you know about what he might have been into, your brother?"

"Drugs," I say softly. "It all spiraled out of control maybe six months ago. Father disowned him and kicked him out of the house."

His eyes narrow. That wasn't what he expected to hear. "*Drugs.* That's what he told you, anyway."

"Hale wouldn't talk to me," I insist. "What else could he have—"

"Time's up." He cocks his head, his eyes steel.

I frown in confusion. "What do you mean?"

Then I hear it. A hush falls through the boisterous crowd, heralding the arrival of a man with wild dark-brown hair and cold brown eyes. I can make out the color from across the room—they're *that* vibrant. Piercing. He targets the brunt of his gaze in our direction, and it seems as though the crowd melts away until he and Daze have nothing but space between them.

"Keaton," the man says by way of greeting. He's tall, about the same height as Daze. He wears a leather jacket paired with dark jeans and a black shirt, but the outfit merely enhances the danger wafting from him. "You have some damn nerve showing up here," he bellows, his voice easily reaching throughout the room.

"Hello to you too, Silas," Daze calls back. He's still hunched over the bar, both of his hands in fists. White knuckles betray just how tightly he has them clenched. I don't know whether to stay or retreat the way everyone else has. I must make a move to stand because Daze looks my way and shakes his head once. *Stay.* Spinning on his stool, he faces Silas directly. "I thought I might be able to make amends."

"After all that high and mighty bullshit you spewed, you still come crawling back on your hands and knees." Silas' voice is soft but no less threatening than my father's when he's in the midst of a powerful sermon. Every word rings with unmistakable influence. Power. "You've always been a jackass, Day, but desperate? That's not like you."

With visible swagger, he approaches the counter from the far end, his arms crossed. The closer he comes, the easier it is to make out the planes of his face, in addition to his eyes. He's older than Daze, I'd guess, maybe mid-thirties. A fresh bruise overlaps a jagged scar that cuts across his right cheek, distorting features that would otherwise be attractive. Now, a corner of his mouth is crooked, as though he's permanently smirking.

"How much do you need this time? Or are you on another bender, and you're too damn high to know when you're treading into dangerous territory?"

"Maybe both," Daze replies, his cocky nature on full display. "Enough to sweeten the memory of sending my fist through your skull the other night." Unfurling to his full height, he stands. "Allow me to make amends. I know for a fact you don't have an excess of fighters. Let me in one round tonight, and my girl will watch. We can call it a truce of sorts. No reason for violence."

"A truce?" Silas cocks his head, his gaze cold. "Oh, no, Day. Traitors aren't entitled to mercy. As far as I'm concerned, you've turned your back on the brotherhood entirely. You want to 'make amends.' Start by leaving town like you swore you would."

"I will, but after one last fight. Name your terms," Daze says, unconcerned by the refusal. "Any stakes you want. One final fight to end things properly. No mess. No grudges."

"Any stakes," Silas murmurs, rubbing his chin. He's drawing out every second on purpose, toying with time. Finally, he shrugs. "Since you were so hellbent on leaving, I want you gone by morning. I want you to stay the hell away from this city—you forfeit *everything*. Though let's be honest, you gave it up months ago. Isn't that right?"

"And *that's* all you want?" Daze scoffs. "I thought you'd be greedier than that, Silas. Here I am on my hands and knees, and all you want is to kick me while I'm down. I was sure you'd go for the jugular instead."

"In good time." Silas smiles. "On second thought, there is one small thing I want to add. Whether you win or lose, you stay the hell away from my nephew. He doesn't need you bouncing in and out of his life whenever you feel like playing the role of father."

I struggle to hide my reaction. Suddenly the hostility between the two men makes sense. This is Sammy's uncle and the man that Daze supposedly attacked on Lyra's doorstep.

"Oh, I got it." Daze shakes his head, chuckling. "Let me tell you what will *really* happen—you can have whatever toys you want to play king. Take my position, take the power, take my money. I don't fucking care. But you stay the hell away from Sammy *and* Lyra. You got that?" Suddenly, he's closer, though Silas doesn't shy away. They stand toe to toe, the visual representation of light and dark. Yin and Yang.

Where Silas is unnerving calm, Daze is all burning rage. "I mean it. Go near him again, and I will fucking kill you," he snarls.

"Oh?" Silas' eyes widen in mock surprise. "Just like you killed his mother?"

FOURTEEN

LIKE YOU KILLED HIS MOTHER.

My throat goes dry as that accusation lands like a nuclear bomb—but if it was meant to throw him off, Daze doesn't blink. Instead, his lips part into a devious grin that transforms his entire face. His eyes seem brighter. Darker. Colder.

And that unsettling, ominous sensation I felt at the door returns in full. It's clear now, more than ever—he's a total stranger.

Someone, I'm not sure I even want to know...

"Yeah." He cocks his head thoughtfully while extending his hand. One by one, he lowers each finger on it, ticking off an invisible list. "I'll kill you like I killed her—fuck your goddamn brains out. Beg you to get clean. Get screwed over, and then watch you fuck up again and again—"

"Like you didn't put the needle in her arm?" Silas takes a step closer, and I stumble back out of pure instinct. They're inches away now, their gazes locked, but an unmistakable tension in the air seems more alarming than the threat of a fight.

It's pure, primal hatred.

"Like you didn't get her pregnant and leave her high and dry?" Silas wonders, his teeth bared. "Some father of the year you turned out to be, too. Not only did you fail the organization that *elected* you leader, but you couldn't even stick around for Samuel—"

"And we both know why that is, don't we, Silas?" Daze bites back.

There's more to what he's said than what's on the surface. Silas' eyes narrow, confirming the suspicion. It was a threat, but in what way? What could keep a father away from his son other than basic neglect?

"Damn," Daze murmurs without elaborating, shaking his head. Another flashing smile adds a chilling contrast to the grit in his tone. "I abandoned him now? You're so busy trying to sniff my shit that you didn't even see what was under your fucking nose. Those new 'friends' of yours? You think someone with that kind of power won't turn on you the second they get the chance? You're playing with fire—"

"That's enough!" Chris slams his hand on the counter, and both men draw back ever so slightly. It doesn't calm my heartbeat, however. I thought Hale and our father could go at it.

But this is something else.

Something violent.

Something, I suspect, that has been a long time in the making.

There's a grim history written in Daze's gaze. Still, he somehow manages to smirk and snatches a freshly-filled shot glass from the counter—courtesy of Chris, I guess. In one go, he downs it all.

"Fuck this," Daze tells Silas after swallowing, swiping his hand across his mouth. "If you want to turn me down, then fine. Let everyone here know as much—" he raises his voice. "And remember whose shoes you're trying to fill. When I was in charge, we didn't rub shoulders with the fucking mob. We didn't deal in hard drugs, and we certainly didn't dabble in the black market. I know what you're really selling these days, Silas, and it isn't the stuff we used to trade in."

Silas holds his gaze, saying nothing. After what feels like a full minute, he pushes past Daze, nudging his shoulder—hard— before heading for a door at the opposite end of the room. On the back of his leather jacket, I spy a breathtaking design. The red-eyed skull sits in the center, among two lines of script spelling out *Westpoint Saints*. It reminds me almost of the jackets Covenant missionaries wear when doing volunteer work. Though, I suspect these men aren't planning on heading to the soup kitchen any time soon.

"Keep telling yourself that," Silas says, his voice drifting back to us. "That you're not a fucking washed-up piece of shit.

That we all aren't better off without you. If you say it enough…maybe you'll fucking believe it. If you change your mind about groveling for scraps, come to Hades. I'll let you play one final time. But on my terms. My rules."

There must be another exit because he storms through the double doors and out of view. A few members of the crowd follow him out, and gradually the previous, lighthearted mood returns as conversation picks up again.

An underlying sense of dread remains, however. I suspect that "fight" was code for something far more sinister than a sparring match.

"Have you lost your fucking mind?" The quiet warning comes from Chris, who nearly lunges across the counter toward Daze. "I thought you wanted to taunt the bastard. Flaunt your presence here—but fight? You do that, and you're as good as *dead*."

"Thanks for the vote of confidence." Daze shrugs himself free but snatches up his bar stool and perches himself on the very edge. "I'm fine. Don't look at me like that. I'm fine!"

"Fine," Chris snaps. Reaching beneath the counter, he withdraws a bottle and slides it across the bar. "But you'll need something stronger. It's on the house."

Daze snatches the bottle and fills his now-empty shot glass to the brim. With a mock salute, he throws it back.

My stomach churns in sympathy.

"Your father would be turning in his grave if he could see you now," Chris remarks. "*Both* of you. The Saints were never the biggest outfit around, but we had pride under him. Respect. If I remember correctly, things weren't too bad under you, either. But now? Your dad would understand your personal troubles. God knows he had his own shit to deal with. But turning your back on the crew? That would be a step too far, even for him, Day."

"I didn't come here for a guilt trip." Setting the glass aside, Daze sighs. "The old man barely had time for me when he was alive. I doubt he cares too much in the afterlife. Besides, last I checked, you aren't exactly a member of the Saints anymore. Are you?"

"Don't be a smart ass." Chris runs a finger along the patch on his sleeve, his eyes narrowing. "Your old man loved you, and once upon a time, he might have been proud of you. *Before* you bowed before Silas and let him turn everything *we* worked for into shit. You may have a death wish, but the rest of us didn't ask to be dragged down with you. And for your information? I was pushed out because Silas only wants yes-men in his crew. I didn't *choose* to walk away, but I'll still uphold the honor of the Saints until my dying day. You used to know a thing or two about that, remember? Honor?"

He storms off to the other end of the bar, turning his attention to another customer.

"What is he talking about?" I demand, fighting to keep my voice level. I fail. "What do you mean by 'fight'?"

"Relax, Blondie," Daze murmurs dismissively. "We just got the invite we were after. Don't get distracted by anything else.

You're here for Hale, remember? I just got us a front row seat to the shit show he tried to warn me about."

He doesn't sound proud of that fact, nor does he seem very excited. Bruised, battered face aside, he looks...

Awful, in a way far beyond the physical. His eyes are cool and empty. Paired with the unusually stern line to his mouth, he could be a different person. Not the intimidating stranger from earlier, either. A man too pathetic to fear. Too desperate.

"What did he mean?" I gather up the nerve to ask. "That you stepped down. That—"

"Forget him," he adds. "All you need to do is pay attention and follow my lead."

"Lead for what?" Goosebumps rise over the flesh of my arms, and my heart beats faster, ramming against my ribcage. Here and now, I realize that mocking, playful Daze is who I prefer. I'd rather have him screw me around for days than look at me like this.

Like...he's drowning, and I'm his only way out.

"You have no idea what you've asked of me tonight," he says, brow furrowing. "It's gonna get rough. The second I look like I'm gonna pussy out—I mean it. I need you to remind me what matters. Do that innocent, virginal thing with your eyes and *make* me remember."

"What?"

"Sammy," he says hoarsely as his hands fall over my shoulders, rooting me in place. His forehead connects with mine, and I swear he's breathing this confession into me as much as he admits it out loud. "*Sammy* is the only person who fucking matters. I can't get sucked in, for his sake. I can't."

Letting me go, he stands up and gently shoves me back, beyond his reach. His arm moves to swipe his empty glass across the counter, and when he looks back at me, he's grinning from ear to ear. It isn't genuine—his eyes are hollow. "You ready to get your answers, Frey?"

"How is a fight going to give me answers?" I ask, my voice rasping.

"Pay attention. Try to see what Hale saw—something bad enough he had to be killed over it." As unease unfurls in my belly, he forms a fist and nudges my chin with it. "But know that I've got your back. No one will lay a finger on you when you're with me. I mean that. Come on, let's go."

He snatches my hand before I can react and hauls me toward the same door Silas exited through. When he throws it open, I realize it leads to a narrow outdoor alley that reeks of piss and garbage from an overflowing dumpster a few feet away.

"Wish me luck, Chrissy," Daze calls to the man behind the bar. Then he yanks me onto the concrete pavement and slams the door behind us.

We walk back to his bike, but he's taking his sweet time—like a criminal doing a perp walk on his way to a life sentence in the slammer.

He moseys along as if savoring the fresh air.

But I know better.

He's putting on a show—deep down, he's angry and itching for a fight.

Or, to put it more bluntly...

He's hungry for blood, and I'm not sure whose.

FIFTEEN

WE RETURN TO HIS APARTMENT, and despite the distance between him and the bar, he hasn't calmed down. If anything, he's even more riled up, pacing the narrow living room like a caged animal while I watch him warily from my seat on the couch.

Things about him stick out to me that shouldn't. How impossibly tall he is, and how beautiful, even at his scariest. My spine is taut with tension as I wait for him to turn all that violent energy on me. For him to rouse that sleepy, primal part of me that all those years of prayer and community service were meant to suppress. He alone brings every dangerous impulse to the surface, and I wonder if this is how Eve felt while gazing at the apple of knowledge.

Like the one thing everyone else told her to run away from, she was compelled to chase. Reach for. Experience in full, no matter the cost. But while Eve's transgression damned the entire human race, the only casualty of my selfishness will be me. The only one damned is *me*.

Being with Daze will destroy me—I know it in my soul. Just as surely as I know that I deserve everything I have coming to me for turning my back on Hale when he needed me most. But the hardest part to reconcile is how much I crave that destruction.

So, I provoke him, though admittedly, I'm not sure why he would take offense to this question. "Who are you, really?"

Perhaps not the deadbeat, carefree person he pretends to be.

"You hinted to Silas that there was a reason you stayed away from Sammy. What is it?"

He whips around, those stormy eyes flashing. After a momentary hesitation, he keeps going, storming into the kitchen. "I'm not in the mood, Frey—"

"I'm not trying to start a fight," I clarify. "I just want to know."

Something in my tone makes him stop short. His back is to me, his head cocked, shoulders radiating tension. "Who am I," he begins in a low tone. All at once, he whirls on me, and I'm paralyzed, rooted to the couch cushions. "Didn't you hear them? I'm a coward. A shitty fucking excuse for a father. A traitor—"

"You helped me," I point out, though I'm not sure if it's meant to counter his argument. Perhaps saving me was yet another crime added to his growing list. He lied to me. Went against Hale's wishes. He lured me into his safe harbor even though he didn't have to.

Why? Out of the kindness of his heart? A part of me scoffs at that. *Of course not.*

"Why?" I ask him outright.

He comes closer, his eyes heavy-lidded, his jaw clenched tight. After observing me for a long moment, he shrugs. "Why not?"

"But that's not it," I say. Feeling bold, I stand up and take a step toward him. What I witnessed in the bar was a mere fraction of the turmoil he feels inside. I used to pride myself on being available to anyone in need. Why stop now? "You wanted something from me," I add. "Didn't you?"

He sighs and rakes a hand through his shorn hair, revealing how uneven a trim it is. "And if I did?"

"I want to help you," I admit. Why? I have no idea. "Tell me what's wrong. I won't judge you. Just talk to me."

"Talk?" He's even closer. Without warning, his hand shoots out, grabbing my chin. It's such a gentle touch that I stiffen in shock. He can be so disarming when he wants to be. So unexpected from the fire and brimstone I'd always believed would follow any sin I chose to commit.

"We can start with why everyone keeps mentioning you being in prison."

His upper lip quirks into a devious smirk, but the amusement doesn't quite reach his eyes. "Almost in prison. I have Silas and your father to thank for that."

I blink. "Because of his campaign?"

"You know what, I don't want to talk," he murmurs, boring his gaze into mine. "Give me your phone."

"W-what?"

He holds out his hand, palm side up. "Trust me." He takes my phone and immediately shakes his head. "No passcode?"

I don't understand the reasoning behind his scoff. "Why would I need a passcode?"

He looks away. Focusing on the screen, he suddenly tenses. After swiping at the screen, he looks up to meet my questioning stare. "I turned your location services off."

"Why?"

"So, you can't be easily tracked."

"What do you mean?"

"And I'm shutting it off," he states, powering it down before placing it inside a kitchen drawer. "To be safe."

I anxiously blink up at him. "Okay."

"So naïve," he sighs, brushing my hair behind my shoulder with his fingertips. "Still want to help me?"

It's a taunt, concealed in a dare, and I feel like we're back in his gym, on the verge of a monumental decision.

"Yes," I say, surprised by how honest the word comes out sounding. "I want to."

Daze steps toward me, backing me against a wall until I'm pinned to it. He towers over me, and I have to strain my neck to look up at him. Without wasting another second, he smashes his lips on mine. His hands roam my body, leaving a warm, tingling sensation in their wake.

I lean into the kiss, fisting his shirt at his chest. A feeling of longing builds up inside me. Being with him just feels *right*. Despite all the many reasons I should be fearful, I feel safe in his presence. Protected.

I shouldn't feel this way.

Daze seems to think so too. He eyes me in such a strange way. It's like he can clearly read every thought in my head, but they just confuse him. Irritate him worse than my speaking out loud had.

"Do you really think you can handle me, Frey?" he asks in a tone that makes my stomach drop through my body and hit the floor. "*Really* handle me?"

I don't think he expects an answer. Without warning, he grasps my waist and yanks me closer. Before I know it, his hands creep toward the hem of my dress, but mine? They fan out over his chest, sensing the coiling muscle twitching beneath his shirt. He makes a low sound at the sensation, and our eyes meet.

"I know what you think of me," he says, and I shudder. Could he really gauge me so easily? "I saw it all over your face back there," he adds. "That I'm a piece of shit. A punk. That I shouldn't be anywhere near someone like you—" He does that thing with my hair again, grasping a chunk of the wig between his thumb and forefinger to twist around. He tugs slightly harder than normal dislodging the wig before tossing it aside to grip my natural hair. When he's done, he doesn't smooth the hair back into place. He lets it dangle apart from the rest. Next, his gaze goes to my cross and stays there. "Maybe I am those things... But you're still here. Still with me. Why is that?"

The potential answer seems to matter to him, though I don't know why. I can't stop myself from fingering my necklace as I mull over a possible explanation and come to a grim conclusion—there isn't one. I'm still here—even when his eyes take on a fathomless quality that makes him resemble the frightening stranger I've only caught glimpses of before now. The real Daze he seems determined to suppress.

For whatever reason, the very enigma of him intrigues me like nothing else. Finally, I say, "Maybe you need me to stay." I can't look at him, and eye the floor instead, still twisting my chain around my finger. "I'm not used to feeling needed."

At least, not by anyone other than Hale, who I failed. The other men in my life would deny such an accusation. Colton would murmur something about both of us only needing prayer, nothing else.

Daze doesn't argue, though. He bites his lip and deliberately flicks my cross with his thumb. It doesn't feel like a dismissive gesture. More like his silent way of answering his own question—this is why you're here. *You're too good. I'm too bad. You can't resist, can you? It's only natural that you want to save my soul.*

"If we do this... We do this differently than before," he says, referring to something far more ominous than mere conversation. "I'm not in the mood for cuddling right now, Frey." His body pulsates with an electric quality. He means that.

But in my limited repertoire of sinful acts, I have no idea what exactly he intends. "How?"

"First, you turn around," he boldly instructs. From his pocket, he grabs an item he must keep on him at all times—a foil packet. One that he expertly rips open with his teeth. "And bend over the couch."

My chest tightens. He's using that guttural, unfamiliar voice again, but it doesn't scare me the way it should. My heart seems to beat faster as if to match the rugged cadence of it. A crazy thought comes to mind—if I were angry and Colton was around, he'd tell me to pray. Meditate. Something as vulgar as sex can't possibly be useful in such a situation, right?

Wrong, at least where Daze is concerned. He seems to thrive on physicality rather than spiritual endeavors. Oddly enough, I can't deny that there may be appeal in his method. When I'm with him, I can't think about anything else. Nothing.

I watch him hook his thumb beneath the waistband of his jeans, eager to take them off.

Ignoring the logical part of my brain warning me to run, I turn around. Then I lean forward and grip the arm of the couch.

"Good girl."

He groans amid the telltale hiss of fabric sliding against skin. The two thumps I hear next must be him stepping out of the material and closer to me. What feels like his hand nudges my legs apart before ghosting up my thigh. He removes the knife first, and my panties follow. Then, his hand returns, wrenching up my dress to brush me intimately with what feels like the broad pad of his thumb. Then the contact withdraws, and a wall of muscle presses into my lower back. Then his hands on my hips. Finally, *him.* He enters me without warning.

The ache between my legs returns in full force, and I still can't get over how I'd been taught this was such an awful sin. How can it be when any pain I feel is followed immediately by pleasure—a harsh, euphoric mixture of the two? His invasion of my body isn't the only sensation I'm reacting to.

It's his touch. He wrenches himself into me, ensuring that there is very little of me he can't contact from this angle. His hand grips the back of my neck, driving me down. Startled, I dig my nails into the worn-out material of the cushions and push back against him, meeting each thrust.

Before, he went slower, letting me adjust to his pace. This time it feels feral. Savage. He takes me punishingly, slamming his hips into mine, seemingly without care if he goes too rough.

At the same time, used and abused isn't what I feel. I feel... Burning heat. Wetness pools between my thighs, and I've never felt so consumed. My back arches, straining the angle he has me in so I can feel more of him. In response, his hand briefly grazes my pelvis before he slips it between my legs, tracing his fingers over the sensitive flesh there. My senses are heightened. I can feel each deliberate touch in a way I never have before. Like his fingers alone drive out any shame or taboo. Groaning, he presses into me, right near where we're joined, rotating his fingers in slow, precise circles.

"So wet," he lets out, slamming into me harder, sending me toppling onto the couch cushions. For leverage, he firmly grasps my shoulder with his other hand, keeping me in place as he drills into me relentlessly. "You like this cock, baby?"

He sounds as unsteady as he moves—as though with every passing second, any semblance of politeness he put on is crumbling. He's vulgar. Primal.

I nod, unable to form words. My face flames at the word choice, but for some reason... I don't take offense to it. The feeling washing through my belly in response feels just as dangerous as the pressure inflicted by his still-teasing fingers. I tilt my head, offering my ear to him, and he nudges the earlobe with his mouth.

"I need you to tell me what it feels like when I fuck you like this. Run that pretty mouth. No one from your precious church can hear you here. It's just me."

I bite my bottom lip to stifle my moans, but they slip out, betraying me.

"Don't be shy," he grunts, leaning his body over mine. Something sharp nips at my earlobe. His teeth? "I want to hear you, Frey. I need to."

There is no explanation to soften the request. My brain plays with it, parsing out a meaning he probably didn't intend. He needs *me* and no one else. Just this feeling. Just my body. Just me. With that thought in my head, he enters me more deeply, grinding his pelvis against mine.

And shock startles me into obeying him. "Amazing," I rasp out. Another moan follows. Then a gasp as he slams into me again. I'm no longer holding back, and the broken, breathless sounds seem to incite something within him. "It feels amazing."

His hand fists through my hair, guiding me to turn my head until I'm staring endlessly into his eyes.

"Yeah?" he asks, grasping more of my hair, pulling tight. In the same breath, he runs his mouth over my shoulder, grating out a command as he goes. "Tell me what you want. Don't pretty it up, either. You give me that honesty you love so much."

There are so many things I could say. Dilemmas that should matter far more than being in this room with him. Should...

"Come on, Frey." He moves again, and my eyelids flutter. At the same time, a sudden tension on my throat makes me glance down. The chain of my necklace is stretched taut, but it takes me a second to realize why—he has my cross trapped between his teeth.

"D-Don't break it," I manage to croak. Then I realize that he's nipping the charm gently, to the point that I could easily pull it free if I wanted. It's such a breathtaking sight—like he has my very soul pinched between his teeth, his to destroy at a moment's notice. He pulls tighter, the chain biting at my skin.

"You wouldn't be the same without it, would you?" he asks, choosing to nuzzle my throat instead. "Sweet little, Frey." Suddenly, he slams into me harder. Again, and again. "Tell me what you fucking want. Loud and clear for the whole damn world to hear."

He thrusts again, and a searing heat tears through my body, robbing me of anything but this. Him.

"You," I hear someone gasp—but that can't possibly be me. Another woman must be responsible, sounding seconds from coming undone. "I just want *you*," she croaks.

And Daze seems to mistake her for me. "Such a good fucking girl," he praises into my skin. He tugs on my hair, drawing my head to the side, which exposes my neck to him. "That's right. Me. So. Take. It. Frey." Brushing his lips along my throat and then shoulder, he sinks into me. "*Every fucking inch of me.*"

He rocks within me, again and again, stimulating parts of me I never even knew existed. I arch my back and match each stroke, creating the perfect rhythm. He makes it so easy to follow him. Chase that insurmountable feeling. That ultimate...

"Do you want to come?" he taunts, once again reading my thoughts. At first, I struggle to grasp what he means. Come? *Oh.* The name for that senseless oblivion that awaits the end of these sinful moments with him. "You're close," Daze adds, his voice taunting as if he knows a secret I don't.

Close. I'm trembling, and so is he. Pulsing. Our bodies are thick with sweat. Breathing is shallow.

"Can you feel it?"

"Yes," I manage to choke out.

"Then beg me." *Thrust.* "For." *Thrust.* "It."

I have no choice but to try. "Please—"

"You can do better than that." His laughter resembles a growl, resonating through my skin in unsettling vibrations. "Beg me."

Another searing thrust robs me of the ability to speak. Gasping, I claw at the fabric beneath me and struggle for clarity.

"Daze—"

"Fucking beg," he commands, eying the dangling chain from my neck before grasping my cross in the palm of his hand and pulling tight.

A terrible thought comes to me, and I'm too breathless to stifle it the way I should. *Forgive me, Father, for I have sinned.*

Again, and again.

"Please!" I desperately moan, wanting nothing more. "Please."

He slams into me harder, firmly gripping my ass cheek with one hand and curving his fingers around my throat with the other. "Try again."

"Please, Daze," I rush out helplessly. "I need this. Please. *Please.*"

"Thatta girl," he groans with amusement. "You feel it now?"

And I do. Like a wave crashing over me, drowning out all sense. All reason.

"I'm—I'm there," I breathe softly as he shifts slightly, planting his palms on the sofa near each side of my head.

"That's it, baby," he urges, quickening his pace. "That's my good little slut. Come all over my cock."

I whimper through a feeling of pure bliss. "Oh, God, yes!"

"Clench your pussy around me, baby. Just like that," he praises, dropping to his elbow, holding me close. "You feel so fucking good. Ah, fuck. Fuck, Frey! *Fuck!*"

His release sounds more violent than mine. He howls and falls forward, crushing me beneath him.

We get dressed in the same clothing we'd been wearing. Him in his coarse jeans and me in my hooker getup, wig included. I wish I could be as collected as he is. Sex seems to do more for him than prayer ever did for me, but I'm not so soothed. My hands are shaking. I can't stop looking over my shoulder just to make sure he actually *is* okay. One glance, and I realize that he isn't. Not really. Just beneath the surface lurks that rage. That unstable anger. He's just better at hiding it now, and with a sigh, he leads the way to the door.

By the time we leave the apartment building, it's dark out, and I'm hesitant to ask where exactly we're headed.

I doubt this "fight" will occur in a mundane location like his gym, given the grim hype placed on it by Chris and Silas. Sure enough, Daze leads me to his bike and silently adjusts the helmet on my head.

Not even ten minutes later, he's pulling into an alleyway surprisingly close to Chris' bar, near yet another seemingly rundown building. Far too soon, we wind up before a battered metal door. Rather than open it, Daze knocks once. At the same time, he grips my wrist so hard I wince. That drowning man comparison floats to the forefront of my mind again—he holds me like he's seconds from going under.

Maybe it's stupid to do so, but I can't stop myself from dislodging his grip in order to grasp his hand, curling my fingers over his. He grips them tight but doesn't look my way once. Instead, he squares his chin and audibly grits his teeth. "Here goes," he hisses as the door opens and someone ushers us in with a gruff greeting.

"So, you decided to show up."

"In the flesh," Daze replies. His shoulders hunch as he steps inside, still tugging me after him.

It's cramped in here. Only the light from outside is enough to illuminate a narrow hallway with a door branching off at one end. Faint commotion emanates from it as the entrance we came through is slammed shut, plunging everything into darkness.

"Silas already had everything set up," the figure who let us in explains as Daze leads me forward, keeping his hand in mine.

"I guess he figured you wouldn't chicken out. I bet that bastard made a pretty penny. I had it two to one that you'd bail. No one shows up to a public hanging for no fucking reason—"

"Hello to you too, Boris," Daze cuts in. He must open the other door because fresh light floods in, illuminating him and the imposing figure beside him. A tall guy with long dark hair and a face that resembles one of the beaten punching mats at Daze's gym. "It was nice catching up," Daze tells him. "But if you don't mind, I have a date."

He tugs me behind him, and I clench my teeth against a complaint. He's actually hurting me now, holding too tight. Way too tight.

Oh yes, he's drowning... But how can I possibly keep him from going under? Especially when I have no idea what exactly he's gotten us into.

"Hey! Watch out, baby."

"Huh?" I blink, registering our surroundings for the first time. I'd been so caught up in my head that I didn't notice the dank hallway switching to a massive room with a concrete floor and a chain-link cage fighting ring in the center.

And people.

So many damn people.

They crowd around rows of metal folding chairs, wearing various versions of dark leather and jeans. Drinking beer and chattering, they barely seem to notice me or the man dragging me along the outskirts of the space.

A tense vibe instantly sets my nerves on edge. Pulsing music seems to resonate down to the foundation of the building, rattling the faded posters taped to the walls. My nostrils wrinkle at the stench of booze in the air. That and sweat. It's like the smell at his gym times a million.

"What is this place?" I have to shout to be heard above the chaos.

Daze grunts without answering as he sidesteps a kissing couple, tugging me along.

"Hey! Daze?"

The voice comes from up ahead, and Daze stops short, so suddenly I nearly run into him. My hand flies out, grasping his arm as I stumble to regain my balance. Before I can, he shifts, pulling me forward, and his arm encircles my waist, hovering way too low.

I'm a bone once again—his alone.

"Hey, Darla," he says as my mind reels. Not for the first time, his change in tone throws me off. It's deep. Cautious. Hostile?

Maybe. But in a very different way than he's confronted Silas. Looking at the slender woman standing before us, I have no idea why.

As horny as Daze pretends to be, he should be drooling.

Not inching away, dragging me with him like a security blanket. My eyes latch onto her hair first—long, blond curls that most definitely aren't a wig. I catch myself self-consciously tugging on the synthetic strands ghosting my shoulders. As I do, the woman eyes my fingers, and her lips quirk.

"Daze," she chirps, drawing his name between a pair of plump, pink lips. "I'm surprised you showed up. Though, I see you have a *new* friend tonight." I choke at the insinuation, but Daze's arm pins me even tighter.

"Yeah," he says. He doesn't look at me, but I can practically hear him telepathically urging me to "play along."

"Oh." The woman's eyes cut in my direction while I focus on her itty-bitty pink tank top and matching miniskirt. A pang of jealousy shoots through me—she has legs for days, coming up to Daze's chin in height. "Shame. I hope you'll still visit me later, though. We used to have such fun, you and I."

My jaw clenches tight. Daze draws me closer.

"Sorry," he grunts, and something flashes across his gaze. An apology? A warning? I'm not given a chance to decipher it before he lowers his head, pressing his mouth to mine. Warmth seeps from his lips as he nudges mine apart with a single flick of his tongue.

Colton would never be so bold. I think that's why I lean into him without thinking it through. Not because I want this. Enjoy this...

Or, perhaps I do, and I'm simply trying to convince myself otherwise.

As if he aims to prove me wrong, he leans in. Applies more pressure. Then he steps into me, gripping my chin with one hand, tilting my head to the side. Held captive in such a way, I can only relent to the onslaught.

He doesn't peck my lips to prove a point—he kisses me feverishly. The way men do in movies—the bad movies I wasn't allowed to watch that had nothing to do with God or the holy tenants my father preaches. Daze is without restraint, without piety. Without morals.

His tongue slips in, perilously deep, but I don't stiffen like I should. I don't bite down. I don't push him out.

I close my eyes and arch my back into him. Fire creeps along my body, recalling his touch. His roaming hands and panting breath. His...

Unexpectedly, he pulls away and shoots Darla a strained version of his charming grin. "I've got plans tonight. See ya around."

He practically shoves me forward toward a corner of the room. Craning my head back, I watch him, trying to decide what that really meant. An act? I should want it to be that simple. I should...

"I owe ya," he mutters as if reading my mind. Is that confirmation that it meant nothing?

"Okay," I stammer, collecting my breath.

"This way." He keeps me close as we weave through the rowdy crowd. Soon enough, we make our way into what appears to be a locker room. Daze shoots a taunting stare at a man smoking something in the corner. "Beat it," he orders.

The other man complies, scurrying out into the hall.

Daze slams the door behind him and rests his palms against the solid, metal frame. He draws in a short breath, his shoulders tensing.

"Are you alright?" I dare to ask, standing helplessly in the center of the room.

"Peachy," he answers smugly before turning to face me. "You want a tour?" He steps further into the room, glancing around. "Lockers," he points out, gesturing to them with a subtle wave of his hand. "More lockers. Some showers. Oh, and a bench."

I raise an eyebrow, unsure as to where this is going. "And taking time to fight someone gets me closer to answers about Hale...how?"

His expression transforms instantly as his mouth loses its playful tilt. "Because the fight isn't what's important. Who's watching? *That* is. It's hard to draw them out these days, the real bastards calling the shots. Seeing me potentially get my ass beaten? That might do it. You just need to pay attention. Look for anyone who shouldn't be here. You'll know when you see them."

"That's cryptic." More so than he usually is. My head swims. Once again, he's speaking in riddles, but I also sense this is one of the most direct things he's said to me. Pay attention. I find myself practicing that command on him first. Despite his apparent bravado, he's still tense with restless energy. Whatever he expects to happen, it isn't good. He's worried. I can't stop myself from reaching out, brushing my fingers along his arm.

"Are you okay?"

"No." He sighs, closing the space between us. "Fuck," he breathes, barely any sound to his voice. I lean into his touch as he cups my face with his hand. "How can I want to bury myself inside you again so soon?"

My lips part, although I remain silent.

He studies me for a while, lightly stroking the contours of my face with the pad of his thumb. "Now she's quiet," he observes, smirking. "I remember when I could hardly get you to shut the fuck up."

"I didn't know you were a liar then," I quip, only to instantly regret it. "I didn't mean that—"

"You did," he counters, but his eyes gleam in a way that makes my chest tighten. A matching smile shapes his lips, and I'm dizzy at the sight. "That's what I like about you, Frey. You're honest as shit. Don't think I don't appreciate it."

"But *you* aren't being honest," I say, feeling bold enough. "Who am I looking for exactly? You keep dancing around the topic. Is that all I can expect from you? Mind games and lies?"

He doesn't take offense. If anything, he seems amused by the banter. Like he's not used to fighting with words—just his fists.

"That's not all you can expect," he says.

Before I realize it, we're closer. My eyes bore into his, and he openly stares back, his head cocked in concentration. All hints of his smirk immediately fade until his mouth is pressed in a firm, straight line. Maintaining eye contact, he inches even closer.

"What you're about to witness isn't going to be pretty," he warns, tracing my lips with his thumb, although I'm too busy trying to silence my thoughts to *truly* hear him. "Are you still with me, Frey?" he asks, tapping my temple. "Get out of that head, will you?"

He makes it sound so easy, though... Around him, it is. I can step outside of myself, if only for a second, and let him fill the empty space grief has left behind. I'm not oblivious to how pathetic that sounds. I think it's why I crave the distraction he provides even more. Enough that I'm here, on the verge of something he seems wary of. Beside him, though, I'm not afraid.

"Yes," I say. "I'm here."

"Good," he sighs, his jaw clenched tight. "Because I need to make sure you understand why we're here."

"Why are we here?"

"You need to keep your eyes open," he instructs. "Don't get lost in the fight like everyone else. You're not here for that. You've gotta dig deeper."

I blink up at him, confused. "I don't understand," I mutter.

"Be aware of your surroundings, Frey. Remember, it's not about the fight itself," he clarifies, lifting my chin to get a better look in my eyes, demanding my complete and utter attention. "It's about *who's* watching. Do you understand?"

I nod.

"Good." He releases a small, shallow breath. "You know... In the glory days, a man's old lady would give him a kiss for luck," he taunts, his smirk on display. "I don't think they teach that in your church, though—"

I think I step into him partly to prove him wrong. Partly out of sheer curiosity. Regardless of the reason, my lips are suddenly on his. From the stillness of his body, it's evident he's just as surprised as I am.

Though my moment of bravery lasts all of five seconds. He's right. I didn't learn that in church. I learned this method of worship only from him. It's spontaneous loyalty. Reckless devotion. It's feeling so vulnerable you can't stand it, and all you can do is try to detract from it.

But he won't let me escape so easily. His eyes darken, lips still pursed.

"I—I'm sorry," I unthinkingly blurt out. "I—"

He moves before I can react, hooking his arm around my waist to bring me against his masculine frame, silencing me with his mouth. Clumsily, my arms find their way around his neck as he lifts me effortlessly from the floor. My heart pumps hard—persistently racing.

I can only hold on for the ride as Daze walks us across the room, pinning my backside to the cold frame of the lockers with a *crash*. Our kiss deepens. It's sloppy, almost a game of wits. Who will back down first? Caught up in a heated moment, neither of us can seem to surrender. Confusion strikes me—however, I push it away.

Nothing else matters.

Not even modesty. To deepen my leverage, I wrap my thighs around his hips, and he slips his fingers beneath my dress, cupping my ass with his hands. My belly dips. Has he already won this round? To my credit, I don't withdraw. He does.

"Don't leave, Frey," he breathes against my mouth, tracing the seam of my lips with the tip of his tongue. "Not until it's over. I need your word on that. Okay?"

"Okay," I whisper. It sounds more like a question than a statement.

Unexpectedly, the door crashes open, and someone barrels inside amid a raucous commotion.

"Fuck off," Daze calls out angrily.

"Time is up," the man states. "Chucky's already in the wings." With that, he hastily shuts the door behind him.

Daze sighs, turning his focus back to me. "Keep your promise." He kisses my lips once more, then drops me to my feet. "Let's go."

He takes my hand, and we exit the locker room. Shoulders squared, Daze weaves us through the crowd. He shifts his gaze to someone behind me—a man standing behind what appears to be a DJ booth, blasting pulsing rock. "I'm here," Daze shouts.

"About damn time!"

Daze laughs in that low, unsettling way as he lets me go and nudges me closer to the console. He wrenches off his shirt and tosses it toward me. I barely manage to catch it, only to find that he's halfway down a nearby aisle by the time my mouth opens for a retort. One look at him, and I bite my tongue. His hands flex in and out of fists at his sides, his head down.

I remember what he said to me in the bar. *How* he said it— *remind me of what matters.*

"Have it your way," the man in the booth mutters, despite Daze already being out of earshot. He shoots me an odd look and then raises a microphone to his mouth.

"You fuckers ready for the fight of the goddamn century?"

Fight. That word lingers in my skull as the crowd roars at the top of their lungs. There must be at least fifty people crowded in this small space. They all jostle for the best seats closest to the ring, reminding me of eager parishioners late to one of Father's sermons.

I doubt they hope to find spiritual enlightenment, however.

They are here purely to spectate whatever will occur in the ring at the center of the space. I'm alarmed to see that Daze's already there, climbing through a chain-link door on the side of the cage. He ditched his jeans and shoes somewhere along the way. Wearing only black boxer briefs, his body glistens beneath the artificial lighting, a beautiful canvas for his numerous tattoos.

"I know you like the buildup, Ladies, and Gents," the man in the booth says to assorted jeers. "But who am I to refuse a legend? Let's get this party started. Who's ready to ruuuuumble?"

More cheers. It's so loud in here I can't hear myself think. My senses can only register bits and pieces of the chaos. Shadow. Light. Noise. Desperate for an anchor, my gaze settles on one of the few stationary people in this damn room—a familiar figure in a corner opposite mine. Silas?

He's fixated on the center of the ring where Daze stands alone, at the mercy of the shouting crowd.

"I *said*—can we hear it for a fucking legend?" the emcee demands. More shouts ring out, and I try to see Daze as if for the first time. He looks older again. Maybe too old, and my lips tingle, remembering the feel of his. At the same time, he looks...

Lost. But not in the way Hale had during those final terrible days. Not in the way I look now. With his eyes narrowed and mouth flat, Daze resembles someone untouchable. The shadowy, enigmatic type of man I'd usually avoid.

Someone dangerous.

A man with nothing left to lose.

To equal fanfare, the other fighter comes from nowhere and lunges into the ring. He's muscular as well, nearly as tall as Daze.

"Let's get this shit started!" The emcee shouts, and the two square off in a circling motion that seems rehearsed. They watch each other rabidly, like wild animals hunting for a weakness in a potential prey item.

Maybe this is a normal occurrence and not a sign of something more sinister to come. After all, I wouldn't know the difference. My knowledge of fighting comes from the few choreographed television fights I watched with Hale back when I shadowed him like a lost puppy. Those brawls had been pretty, painstakingly structured. Almost like a dance.

That comparison shatters when Daze's opponent lunges and slams a punch into his ribcage. This is no charade designed solely for entertainment.

This is messy.

I lean forward, my eyes bug wide. I think I must cry out because Daze's eyes cut in my direction. In the same motion, he betrays a predatory grace that allows him to pivot on his heel to avoid another punch. Mid-motion, he slams his own fist into the other man's shoulder. Flesh connects with flesh with a sickening thud—again, reinforcing the brutality of this event.

It's not faked. Neither man holds anything back.

Daze's opponent lunges, trapping him against the chain-link fence as the crowd roars its approval. Dear Lord. I'm sick to my stomach, unable to tear my gaze away. I feel like I'm in ancient Rome during biblical times—in the coliseum, a witness to unfathomable violence. A vicious spectacle.

An arena awash in blood. Red drops fly from Daze's mouth as he catches a blow to the face, and I wince in sympathy. As he sways on his feet, I fear that he might have lasting damage, like a concussion.

And it bothers me. It frightens me.

Before I can fully think the thought through, I cry out consciously this time. "Daze!"

Head cocked, he stiffens, dodging another punch, and I cry in relief. Then he twists at the waist, and holds his own with a retaliatory strike.

Yes! I pray it's over, but the crowd around me roars. This was just an appetizer, it seems. Suddenly, the mood seems to shift, and I come to a grim realization—what little civility existed before now quickly descends into chaos.

The two men lock eyes, and it's like they leave the world for their own dimension. One where they can't hear the shouting or see the spectators cheering wildly on their feet as they start trading blows in a whirlwind flurry.

They're beyond the whims of mortal men. They're demons in a battle fit only for the depths of Hell.

And amid that breathtaking carnage, it quickly becomes apparent that Daze is the one throwing the most punches that land. As if feeding off the successive hits, he pummels his opponent ferociously, backing him against the opposite side of the cage, pinning him near a corner pole.

Around me, the crowd swells, and distinct shouts punctuate the deafening cheers. "Finish it! Finish it! Yeah! Beat the shit out of that fucker!" Eventually, it grows into a chant.

Finish. Finish. Finish...

It's a demand Daze seems to feed off, punching faster. Harder. The sounds become more violent. Crunching noises mingle with the pounding impacts. He rocks back and forth with every new attack. Almost instantly, sweat slicks his body, flattening his newly-shorn hair close to his scalp. He looks more animal than human.

A monster.

As I watch, his words echo in my skull. *It's gonna get really rough, and the second I look like I'm gonna pussy out—I mean it. I need you to remind me what matters.* In his lingo, I don't think he meant "pussy out" by losing this fight.

"Daze!" I slink forward, weaving through people clamoring for a better view. My height plays to my advantage for once, and I manage to inch closer to the ring. Close enough to almost taste the sweat and hear the violent grunts interspersed with every thudding blow. "Daze!" My voice sounds raw, but I barely make a dent in the raucous din.

He can't hear me.

Blind to reason, he becomes ruthless. His opponent curls, any moment from forfeiting. Without thinking, I call out. Scream. "Hey! Daze! Daze—"

He stiffens, and his opponent lands a desperate glance off his chin, making him stagger back. Instantly, he turns, his eyes finding mine, and I suck in a breath. His eyes narrow, ruthless, and cold. I'm frozen, too stunned to speak. All I can do is force my lips into a silent reminder. *Sammy.*

He recoils, shaking his head as if clearing it. A glimpse of the man who comforted me the other day returns. I *see* him. Then his opponent regains his balance, and he doesn't even attempt to block the punch aimed at his chest. Another blow, and he goes down hard on his knee.

My heart pounds viciously against my ribcage.

My ears begin ringing.

This should be enough, right? He's down, unmoving. The fight should be over. It should be enough. It should...

The man towering over him delivers a kick to his stomach, and I'm defeated by the hungry roars that rise in response. Daze groans, his mouth contorted in agony. Rather than savor his victory, the other fighter doesn't let up, punching him again. Again.

"Daze!" I surge forward, jostling for a closer position to the ring and I'm almost instantly shoved back. When he scans the nearby spectators, he can't see me—but he looks. I can see the confusion on his face. The anger warring with building rage.

That should be enough. He did his job. The fight should be over.

But it isn't. When Daze staggers to his feet, his opponent comes for him again. Instinctively, Daze rams his head into the man's chest, knocking him off balance. Together, they collapse into a heap of flying blows, but it's different this time. There is no push and pull before Daze takes charge with ruthless efficiency.

My God, he's terrifying. There is something beautiful in how his body glistens beneath a layer of sweat and blood. How he fights so hard, he's shouting with the force of every blow. He's unstoppable—a mountain of flesh that will crush anything foolish enough to block his path.

Even if that obstacle is another human.

"Holy fuck," someone exclaims nearby. "I think we're gonna see a bloodbath tonight, you poor fucks."

A bloodbath. Daze is already covered head to toe in it. I have enough sense of mind to realize that it isn't all his. It can't be. It's mainly coating his fingers. His hands.

Then his face as he strikes his opponent's head, and droplets of crimson go flying.

My heartbeat surges. I feel sick. It's as if a part of me realizes what's happening before it actually does.

The other fighter goes limp, but Daze doesn't stand over him in triumph of his victory. He scrambles on top of him and keeps going. Hitting. Punching.

"Enough!" The speaker repeats himself several times, but even a crowd as riled as this one seems to race to quiet in the wake of his voice. When I follow the sound, I see why.

Silas stands near the ring, his eyes blazing. "Enough. Get him the hell out of there," he snaps.

Two men lunge into the ring through the chain-link door and grab Daze by his shoulders. It seems to take their combined strength to finally draw him off from an opponent who is no longer moving.

He can't, a voice in my head whispers. He won't be moving ever again. His head is too misshapen. Too bloody. His neck shouldn't be at such an odd angle...

Amid the shouting, screaming crowd, Daze pushes away from Silas' men and stands, trembling, on his own two feet.

The emcee doesn't even bother to announce him the winner. Instead, the man climbs into the ring through the makeshift door and raises Daze's fist before he pushes away and storms from the ring entirely.

Silas moves to follow him, his shouts audible even from here. "What the fuck, Daze? You agreed to every term, remember? That you'd go down silently," he snaps. "You think you can pull a stunt like that and walk away? What the hell is wrong with you—"

"I told you I was coming for you," Daze shoots back before staggering to my end of the ring, covered in blood. "Try and stop me, and you'll end up the same fucking way."

He vanishes in the direction of the locker room, but I can't follow. I can't move at all. Finding Hale was the worst experience of my entire life, but this comes close.

I can't wrap my head around it all. I've just watched him take a man's life so easily... Without a shred of guilt. How could he be the same man who stopped me from jumping?

How can he be so brutal in one instant, yet so caring with me in another?

What does he want from me?

It's just too much.

Dazed, I turn on my heel, barreling for the door. It feels like an eternity of pushing past heavy, unfamiliar bodies before I finally break free near the outskirts of the room. Only now can I register the shock and fear that leave me sick in their wake. I'm going to throw up soon. I know I will.

On the verge of gagging, I spy a metal door that I hope leads outside, and I lunge for it. I need fresh air. I need to leave. I need to pray for my soul and hope to never witness something like that again.

"Wait!" Apparently, the devil won't let me go so easily. Someone grabs my arm from behind, and I know who it is from his smell alone.

"Please," he grates against my ear. "Frey, hear me out. That wasn't... Just talk to me—"

"No!" I wrench away from him as hard as I can, but he's too strong—even though his hand is so wet. "Let go of me!"

"Let her go," a rough voice calls out. Ben? I don't see him in front of me, and I don't have the strength to look behind. "Let her go, Day."

He must listen because a second later, I break away and stagger blindly into a thinning group of people nowhere as thick as near the ring. I put all my focus into pushing past them. I barely hear the voice that calls out.

"Frances? Frances?"

It isn't Daze, but my head whips around with chilling recognition. That voice doesn't belong here. Not in a den of vice and violence.

A glance over my shoulder reveals just blurred, unfamiliar faces, and I turn back for the door, convinced I'm hallucinating. Panicking. Then I see him. A face blurred by movement but still recognizable enough to send a chill through me. Dark hair. Darker eyes. The hallmark traits of a man who rarely leaves my father's side, if ever—one of his most trusted acolytes. Robby.

Fear drowns out any logical reason for why he could be here. Wherever Robby is, my father isn't far behind. Panicked, I turn back for the exit, and at this stage, I don't waste time being polite. I push and shove my way forward until I make headway.

Somehow, I wind up outside, running down the street without looking back. I don't have my cell phone. Then a hysterically horrifying realization comes to mind—I left it at Daze's apartment. Without it, I don't even know where exactly I am.

Or why an agent of my father's would be here as well. Robert O'Neil. Though I may have imagined him—or more simply, Father had me followed all this time. Somehow the prospect isn't as terrifying as the thought of Daze finding me. Touching me with bloodstained hands. Convincing me that what I just saw hadn't actually happened.

I can't.

So I just run.

SIXTEEN

FATHER BROKE down after a full year of pleading and let me move into my apartment. After Hale died, I barely slept there, staying in my old room instead, next to his.

He was the reason for the spare key I keep hidden under the welcome mat. Sometimes he'd visit before things got truly bad. When I fish it out now, the pain nearly desolates me. I wind up leaning against the door, fighting to unlock it through a haze of tears.

Once inside, I climb into the shower and sit with the water running as I try to process everything that's happened.

The first realization to come to mind? Daze is a murderer. Did he kill Hale as well? He might have, and I didn't see the obvious warning signs. Hale's drawing wasn't meant to high-light Daze as an ally but as an enemy. He's dangerous.

And I slept with him. I let him inside my body more than once. I...enjoyed it.

Overcome by emotion, I bolt upright and throw up in the toilet—but it isn't enough to lessen the nausea ripping through me.

The truth is, no matter how righteous I may feel now, I'm no better than he is. All I can do is punish myself by delving deeper into the questions I've tried to avoid dwelling on before now. Why did Hale draw that symbol? Was he there at that place? Did he witness a similar fight? Is that what drove him to the brink?

I can't put the puzzle pieces together on my own, and the failure guts me. What was he afraid of? Maybe the answer is obvious. He told Daze to stay away from me for a reason. He was there waiting for me at the bridge for a *reason...*

And he might be in this very apartment right now, having followed me home.

The sound of knocking penetrates through the rushing water. I spy the handle of the knife sticking out from the pile of clothing on the floor and lunge for it.

Still naked, I grab a towel and creep to the door, holding my breath. My hand shakes so badly that I can barely keep it brandished in front of me while gripping the towel around me. Do I have it in me to hurt someone?

The answer comes to me as if whispered into my ear by a voice suspiciously similar to Daze's. *Hell no, you don't.*

As the knob turns, the doubt grows. Still, I raise the blade higher. "Who's there?" I ask.

The door opens fully, revealing a shadow on the other end.

Fear paralyzes me. All I can do is croak, "Stay back!"

The intruder doesn't listen, boldly stepping inside the foyer, his face bathed in shadow. When his voice comes, it's cautious. Familiar... "Frances?"

"C-Colton!" I blink, too stunned to lower the weapon. Struck dumb, I gape as he flips on the hall light, his expression puzzled. "Goodness! What are you doing here?" I ask.

He raises an eyebrow while eying my damp towel and dripping hair. "Are you okay?" He starts forward, but something in my expression makes him stop short and raise his hands in a placating motion. I also notice that he has the decency to avert his eyes away. "I was worried about you. You haven't been answering your phone, and I thought it might be prudent to stop by with all the drama around the explosion."

"What—How did you get in?"

"Are you okay?" he asks, avoiding the question entirely.

Alarm bells go off in my mind, but I focus on his question rather than my unease. Am I okay? No. I'm not.

"I... I was showering," I croak out before rushing back toward the bathroom.

Colton follows, his tone more concerned. "Frances? Did something happen—"

"I'm fine!" He gains on me far more quickly than I expect, and I barely manage to make it inside before I smell his cologne and sense his nearness. "I'm fine!" The knife clatters to the floor as I slam the door in his face.

Then, suddenly, it hits me.

A rush of pure adrenaline. Confusion. Anger.

I burst back into the hallway and am met with a pair of shocked, wide eyes once I enter the living room.

"You need to leave," I tell him sharply. "Now."

"Are you okay?" Colton steps toward me. "Frances—"

"You can't just barge in like that, Colton. That isn't okay." I strive to make my voice resemble something calm. I think I fail, judging from the way he gapes at me. Like I've just grown two heads.

"You seem upset," he says, reaching for my hand. "I really think we should talk—"

"Get out, please—"

"We should pray." He keeps coming, cinching my hand in a slightly tighter grip. "You're stressed. Let me help you confess any sins you may have. Sit down with me."

The command snaps something inside of me. Confess my sins? There are far too many to name. Sex out of marriage. Witnessing a murder. Sleeping with said murderer. Interacting with Daze. Daze. Daze. The shame, pain, and fear descend all at once, and something dark and mean unfurls within me. Before I can even rationalize the action, I feel my lips part.

"Get out of my apartment!" That wasn't my strained, controlled tone. That was a scream. Still, once it's out of my lungs, I can't seem to regain control. "Now, Colton! Get out!

Get out!"

"Okay!" He scurries off, glancing over his shoulder as I follow him to the door.

"Frances—I don't understand—" he begins, pulling open the door before stepping out into the hallway.

"I will call you tomorrow," I snap. "When I'm ready. Just...give me time. Thank you."

With that, I shut the door in his face.

And I lock it.

Wondering if even that will suffice.

Daze was a liar in many ways, but he had been right about one thing—I can't trust anyone.

Especially not him.

I don't know how I managed to sleep. I wind up taking a shower, embracing the steaming water as it scorches my skin until the hot flow eventually runs cold. Afterward, I do my best to mentally prepare myself for Colton's questions as I get dressed in a sweater and skirt—and beneath it, I strap on Daze's knife, oddly reassured by its weight. Once I'm ready, I head for the living room, and as if on cue, a gentle knock sounds from my front door.

"It's me," Colton calls from the other side of the doorway. I inhale a small breath before removing the chair I had used to barricade it last night to keep out all unwelcomed visitors. I open it slowly. In his hands are two steaming cups of coffee, one of which he hands to me. "I figured you could probably use some caffeine."

"Thanks," I mutter, accepting the coffee as I step aside. He watches me take a tentative sniff, and I try to think of the first question I can ask—anything to avoid what happened last night. "How is Salvation? I hope the damage wasn't too great."

"No, but the main building is still under investigation," Colton explains. "First, let's sit."

He heads into the living room, and I follow him, claiming the seat beside him on my small beige couch. We've been here before, seated far closer than this. But...

In those moments, I remembered feeling a calming, slightly pleasant warmth. Today, the energy from him makes me feel cold. I shiver, and he places his hand on my thigh.

"Are you okay?" he asks.

I flinch back and shift to the other end of the couch. "I'm fine," I say.

With a frown, he lets his hand fall and clears his throat. "I've been really worried about you, Frances. Especially after what happened last night. Can you explain why you were so upset?"

I know the innocent, fearful type of answer he expects, but the wrong words spill out of my mouth. "You broke into my apartment. Why wouldn't I be upset?"

"Broke in," he echoes, shaking his head dismissively with a grin. "I'd say that's a bit overdramatic—"

"Is it?" I ask although it's obviously rhetorical. "Because I don't remember ever giving you a key."

His jaw clenches tight. "It was unlocked, Frances."

No. It wasn't.

I was so hellbent on being alone and making sure nobody could get in that I vividly remember checking the lock multiple times before I went into the shower.

"Besides," he adds pointedly. "Given the state of our relationship, I think we're beyond asking for a calling card to visit, don't you?" He reaches for my hand and runs his thumb across my palm.

My heart sinks, and the dreadful feeling I felt last night settles back in.

He's lying.

Why is he lying?

"I do think I deserve an apology," he adds, his gaze on my fingers. "You slammed the door right in my face. You were so angry. Don't worry, however. I forgive you."

Tears well up in my eyes, although it's not from sadness.

I can't quite decipher the wave of emotions that rushes over me. Fear? Disgust? Maybe even betrayal?

He hadn't come here out of concern for me, I suspect. He'd been told to. By my father? He'd been so hellbent on fulfilling his task that it hadn't even crossed his mind to ask for permission to enter my personal space. Fighting back tears, I fake a grin.

"You're right," I lie, giving in. "I'm sorry."

He smiles. "Don't worry about going back to work just yet. For now, we'll be operating out of the satellite office on the other side of town. You don't have to come—"

"No," I say over him. "It's fine."

The truth is, I need to get out of here. I feel trapped, yet I'm unsure where to go. I'm not ready to face Daze yet, yet the last thing I want to do is be alone in my apartment with Colton. He's lying. They're all lying.

At this point, the only one who isn't lying to me anymore is Daze.

After coming to the realization that doing mindless work at Salvation to clear my mind is the best option I have, I smooth my hands over my sweater and nod.

"I'm ready," I tell him. "I can do whatever is needed. We can go now."

"Are you sure?" His tone is relentlessly calm, but I bristle at it. After last night, I could be paranoid, but it doesn't quite sound like him, reaching out to me only from a place of concern. He sounds like my father, always probing. Hunting for a sign of weakness. Disobedience. Sin.

Far away from the horror of the fighting ring, I let myself replay the voice I heard and the image I saw as I was leaving. Had my father's operative truly been there after all? Had I imagined it? Is Colton here by chance, or to confirm whatever suspicions were aroused by the sight of a woman who looked like me far from where she should be?

Rather than give anything away, I nod. "I'm sure. Let's go now."

I raise my cup of coffee and instinctively freeze when the lid touches my lips.

Colton frowns, watching me closely. "Frances?" he questions. "Is something wrong?"

Yes, the voice in the back of my head screams, *something is very wrong*. Daze's words keep echoing off my skull. *Trust no one. Not them. Not them.*

"It's too hot," I reply swiftly, setting the cup aside. "Let's go."

With that, Colton stands and heads for the door.

And unlike him, I leave my coffee behind.

Colton drives me to the office and the morning unfolds like any other. I don't see any obvious signs of nefarious activity. Daze and Hale were both wrong.

At least I try to convince myself of as much.

As Colton and I set about our daily tasks, nothing horrific pops out of the woodwork. If anything, the next few hours pass uneventfully. We help out in the kitchen and pass out materials to the homeless who gather in the courtyard outside.

It's relatively monotonous, much like the days before Hale's death. I'd give anything to return to that time and listen to him, no matter how insane his rants sounded. I'd listen to every word. My support alone might have been enough to prevent any eventual tragedy from unfolding.

"There is something I should tell you," Colton says mere minutes before our lunch break. "I didn't want to warn you off. I think it's good for you to get out today. But...your father is scheduled to stop by."

I don't know how to process the emotion washing over me. Alarm? Dread? Relief?

I say nothing, instead grabbing a mop from the back of the kitchen. "I'll clean up," I say, forcing a smile.

"I'll be outside, handing out pamphlets."

He heads off, and the second he's out of sight, the composure I've held until now breaks. My knees buckle, and the mop alone is what holds me up.

I swipe the same few tiles over and over again, desperate to find the peace of mind cleaning usually gives me. Instead, I'm reminded of being in a small, filthy apartment piled high with beer cans. I can still see Sammy, blissfully engrossed in his favorite cartoon. I can almost feel that inexplicable calm I haven't felt since I left. It's not fair that he could make me feel safe there, among squalor and sin.

It's not fair that, after everything I've seen, I can't get his face out of my head. Or the image of him standing over a man beaten into a bloody pulp. Dead.

He didn't look fierce then. Just terrified.

I can't put off this meeting forever. He finds me first, venturing into the break room, which seems so plain compared to his tailored, navy suit and perfectly-coifed graying hair. In the doorway lurks a figure who remains in the hallway, but his presence affects me, nonetheless. Robby. Did he see me last night? Was he really there? Or was it a figment of my imagination?

I don't even want to consider the possibility, and, as if to taunt me, something Ben said haunts me now—*You think Daze and I are bad news? What about that little bootlicker who follows your father around? Robert something? That guy is the real danger you should be worried about.*

"Frances?" Father is watching me, his head cocked in confusion.

I scramble to force a smile. "F-Father."

I should be prepared to face him—but I'm not. Shock makes me drop the mop handle, which skitters across the floor.

"I've been worried sick about you." He draws me into a hug, and the familiarity stings. "Where have you been?"

"I... I was at a friend's house."

He raises an eyebrow. "Oh?"

"Someone I met through our outreach. I was safe."

"Frances..." He frowns and folds his hands together in the pious way he does before every sermon. As if he needs his full strength to deliver his next words of wisdom. "You should be careful. It is a tenant of our faith to be trusting, but one must also be wary of those who are not members of our flock."

Like Daze Keaton, former member of a gang of criminals. Still, I technically didn't lie. For all intents and purposes, I met him through Hale.

"I was safe with them, Father. But I'm sorry for worrying you."

He accepts the apology with a nod, but his eyes linger over my face as if hunting for any sign of deception. Fear unfurls in my belly. Does he know the truth about where I've been? From his watchful stare alone, I can't tell. "I know this has been hard on you. Given how tight this race is, we can only afford to show our family's resilience, no matter the tragedy that befalls us. That can't be easy." He reaches out, placing the flat of his palm over my forehead. It's the gentle way he used to placate me when I was a child, and one touch from him could quiet even my worst fears. "I couldn't bear it if anything happened to you."

"I'm sorry," I say. More doubt creeps in, along with fresh guilt. I spent so long wanting to believe there was some truth in Hale's obvious mistrust. What if I'd been wrong? What if he had just gone off the deep end like everyone said?

While he changed, Father has remained the same unwavering paragon of authority he's always been. That should count for something.

"There is another thing I wanted to discuss with you, Frances," Father continues, lowering his hand. "You haven't answered your phone. Even Colton couldn't get a hold of you, it seems."

Because I don't have it. Does he know that? My lungs constrict, and I can't suck in enough air. His face doesn't transform into the stern, cold frown he wears when displeased, however.

"I... I left it home," I lie. Every trembling word seems to betray me, but he merely raises an eyebrow.

"That isn't like you."

I say nothing. *Does he even know you?* some rebellious part of me whispers. It wasn't always there—I think Daze is responsible for this newfound part of me, tempting me to question everything. Even my own father.

"I've just been...stressed," I say finally. "I'm sorry."

"I know," he says. It's the right phrasing, but his tone has no emotion. Certainly not the level of grief I still feel when it comes to Hale. He sounds mildly understanding as if we were speaking about the weather. "We've all been drained by current events, I think. You should come home tonight, and we'll have dinner and talk. Just the two of us. And Colton if you'd like. He cares a lot about you."

I wait for him to caveat the offer with a request that I go to Covenant right now and confess my sins. He has to know... Right? If he had me followed, he'll have his doubt.

Or, a more terrifying thought comes to mind—he doesn't know. Robbie wasn't there for me.

"Frances?"

I startle to awareness and nod. "Okay."

"We are all concerned for you, darling. Tomorrow, I think you should come to the service. It might do you some good."

I say nothing, but my strained smile seems to be the only response he needs.

"I'll let you finish up." After planting a chaste kiss on my cheek, he leaves, but the relief I thought I'd feel doesn't come. Just more pain. More unease. Both fester among the doubt sowed by Hale's drawing. Why did he leave that for me to find?

After one last pass over the floor, I return to the main lobby and spy Colton standing on the sidewalk before a small crowd. A few potential converters have already strayed inside, scanning the framed portraits of various Salvation missions.

I should feel pride in his success, but I'm just anxious to leave and parse over my thoughts in peace. With a sigh, I step toward the doorway and run into someone approaching from my side.

"Excuse me," they say.

I force a smile and keep moving. "It's okay—" Belatedly, I register the familiar, guttural cadence of their voice. I smell him next. Instantly, I know this man is no stranger.

It's *him*. Daze—but when I whirl to face him, he's far from the malicious figure I've built him up to be in my head. He's tired and battered, swaying on his feet. A gray woolen cap shrouds his head and the wound I know to be there, but there is no disguising his black eye or the cuts along his lip.

"Hear me out," he warns, his tone low. "You think I'd come here if I wasn't worried about you? You aren't safe here—"

"Like you know anything about safe," I spit.

The cold, icy Daze would smirk in response. Instead, he... Winces. My heart pangs. By my side, my fingers twitch toward him, but I shake my head and force them down.

"Go away."

"I'm sorry, Frey," he begins, his voice low. "I know you're pissed at me, and I'm sorry you had to see that shit, but it was the only way I could get you your answers—"

"What answers? I still don't know what happened to Hale or why," I shoot back. "You need to leave. Now."

His eyes darken, but rather than grab me, flash a weapon, or otherwise live up to his darker persona, he shrugs. "Fine." Turning his back to me, he heads for the side exit before spinning back around, determined. "You asked why I was at the bridge that day, but what you really should question is why I would break a promise to a dead man and approach you in the first place. Right then? You needed me. Even Hale's request couldn't keep me away from you. If you need me again, I'll be there. You know where to find me."

He's gone before I can even get a word in edgewise, though I'm not sure what I could even say. Perhaps that I didn't need him? I had been fine on my own, isolated in grief, unable to ask anyone else in my life for help. To the extent that I emotionally unloaded on the first stranger to offer me a chance to speak. The first person to actually listen to me.

That doesn't mean I needed him. It doesn't.

"Frances?" I startle and look up, unaware that Colten had even come in. "Are you ready to leave?" he asks.

"Yes," I say thickly.

Did he see Daze? From his face alone, I can't tell. Still, an uneasy feeling sinks into my stomach and won't leave. I try desperately to push these feelings away, but alarm bells begin ringing in my head, becoming louder and louder with each passing second. Until, suddenly, they're *screaming*.

How can I watch Daze kill a man and still feel entirely safe in his presence, yet being anywhere near Colton only seems to set off warning signals in my brain?

I'm now on guard, questioning everyone's motives.

It's as if the closer I get to the truth, the more none of this seems to make sense.

"Actually... I'd like to take a walk first," I tell him, backing away. "I need to clear my head. I'll call you later."

"For dinner," Colton says, leaving the request as nonnegotiable. "Your father would like us at his home. So, we can talk."

"Yes," I stammer, heading for the door. "I'll be there."

Though I can't escape the feeling that it didn't seem like a typical family meal. There is a significance to it that I can't decipher. To talk about my relationship with Colton? Perhaps he wants to move things along and took it upon himself to approach Father directly.

Or...

The man I heard last night was no figment of my imagination. Father's own agent was there at the ring, and if he wasn't following me, then why...

SEVENTEEN

I WALK FOR BLOCKS, but I don't wind up in front of my apartment in the safe, upscale part of the city. I blame the turmoil of my thoughts for wandering so aimlessly. I can't stop seeing Daze. His face. Those eyes. I can't silence his voice, echoing ceaselessly in my skull.

You think I'd come here if I wasn't worried about you? Worried about you. Worried. You...

I should be glad to have a reason not to trust him. According to my faith, only Father is worthy of such an honor—him and the man he chooses for me. Colton.

But Daze persists, easily drowning out their concerns. *Don't trust them*, he told me before. *No one.*

But that's exactly what a devious sinner would say to tempt me to further corruption.

You needed me. If you need me again, I'll be there. You know where to find me.

And maybe I'm of such weak moral character that it works. When I finally take stock of my surroundings, I'm not surprised by what I find. I'm near a familiar rundown gym, though I'm not sure how I found it. Found him. He's in the alley, leaning against the brick wall, smoking a cigarette. He pauses mid inhale when he sees me. Despite his bravado, I don't think he actually expected me to come.

Slowly, he lowers the cigarette and then tosses it, stamping out the embers with his boot. Tilting his head my way, he merely nods before heading toward the street. While my arrival came as a surprise, he seems to know I'll follow him. He doesn't look back, though I keep my distance, and I'm sure he can't see me in his peripheral vision.

We don't talk until we finally reach his apartment, and he ushers me inside.

"Fuck." He collapses onto the couch, and I find myself rushing to the sink and pouring water onto a rag. Giving him first-aid seems to be second nature to me now. I return to him and crouch down before applying the rag to the worst of the injuries—his left eye.

"You're lucky you're even conscious," I blurt out as slivers of sunlight illuminate his face in stark relief. "That was..."

I can't even put the level of violence into words. Frankly, I'm surprised he's able to move at all. Though, at least he still can. His opponent wasn't so lucky, and I shiver at the thought that the very hands braced over the couch cushions had taken someone's life mere hours ago.

"I'm resilient, baby," he groans in response. His hand captures my wrist as his eyes meet mine. One of them anyway —the other is swollen shut. "Thank you, by the way. Thanks."

I adjust my grip on the rag and apply more pressure. "For what? Watching you nearly get beaten to death? For not calling the police? For letting you play me for a fool?"

"For trusting me," he says, letting his hand fall. "You wouldn't be here if you didn't. I... I didn't want you to see that. I mean it."

"Why did you do it?" I demand.

He flicks his gaze away from me, eyeing the wall. "Do what?"

"Seriously?" I snarl, taking in a sharp breath. "You killed someone! Don't try to deny it. I know what I saw."

Blood and gore and ruthless violence.

"Admit it," I rasp. "You want me to trust you? Then say it. I mean it, or I'm gone."

"Fine..." He turns his gaze to the ceiling, his mouth contorted in a grimace. "I had to, Frey," he states strongly. "I had to."

"What do you mean?" I poke him as his eye drifts shut without him answering me. "Hey!"

"It was a setup, Frey." His eyelid lifts, and our gazes meet. A pulsing sensation shoots through me, but I try to ignore it. I *have* to ignore it. "Silas, that gutless coward. He wanted me dead. When it came down to it... It was either his pawn or me."

I want to deny it. Murder can't be as easy as self-defense. Right? That has to be a cop-out. But then I remember...

"I saw him," I admit out loud, frowning at the memory. "Silas. He was watching when... When the man wouldn't stop while you were down."

"I'm not surprised," he says with a cold laugh.

"Is that what you wanted me to see?" Even as I ask the question, an answer comes to mind. No. He told me to pay attention to the other spectators. In the moment, I'd been too distracted by the fight to truly notice those around me. One figure, however, stands out. "I think I saw..."

"Who?" he asks when I trail off.

But I don't even know how to say it. That one of my father's men had been on the sidelines—not because he'd been following me, but... Why else?

To watch Daze potentially be killed?

It's far too dangerous a suspicion to voice out loud. So, for now, I say nothing.

Daze winces, his eyelids fluttering. "Fuck. I need to sleep."

I'm not sure if I should let him. Though it isn't like I have any other options. Within seconds, he starts snoring—or choking on his own blood for all I know.

All I can do is treat him with what little first-aid supplies I scrounge from his narrow bathroom. Which isn't much. A roll of gauze and a few cotton pads are the best excuse for a bandage I can come up with. The superglue as well, considering all his wounds are deep enough to need it. When I finally finish, he's deep asleep, slumped on the couch in a lazy posture that resembles someone taking a cat nap.

Not a guy battered and bruised with blood seeping through his fresh dressings.

"Dear God..." I tug at my cross and wrestle with another impulse to take him to a hospital. Call an ambulance.

Or just leave. He could die, and I can't handle that again. Seeing a body. Touching it, searching for signs of life...

I *can't* do that again.

An arrogant prick even while unconscious, Daze grunts as if to reassure me. The bastard is too stubborn to die. At least for now.

So, I sink onto the floor beside the couch and brace my back against it. My eyes drift shut as I listen to the steady cadence of his breathing. At least if he does die, there is one bright side.

At least I didn't leave him alone.

EIGHTEEN

I WAKE up to the sensation of someone running their fingers through my hair. Shock ricochets through me, and I wrench my eyes open, hope in my throat. For a second, I forget...

But the figure watching me warily isn't my brother.

"Rise and shine, Freylie Frey," Daze says. God, he sounds awful. He looks it too. His face is a smorgasbord of purplish bruises and dried blood. Still, he attempts what I can only assume is a smile.

"Holy crap," I whisper, blinking back the remnants of sleep. "Are you sure about that hospital?"

"I feel peachy keen," he says gruffly. He's still lying flat, his head turned as far in my direction as he seems able to tolerate. Wincing, he tries to smile. "Better than that, even, considering the view." He rakes his gaze down to my hip, but the expression lacks his usual bravado. He looks more agonized than lustful. "You have pretty green eyes, you know that? Even if you have four of them—"

"That's it!" I haul myself upright and turn to face him. From this height, I tower over him, and the idea of it is oddly thrilling. His bulk dominates the couch leaving no ounce of space for me to occupy if I feel the urge to sit beside him. He watches me without moving as I wave my fingers in front of his face. "How many am I holding up?"

His good eye squints. "Twelve."

I turn on my heel and scan the room for his cell phone. "I'm calling 911—"

"Relax!" He coughs, and I hear the couch cushions squeal with movement. "It was a joke."

I flinch as his hand snags mine before I can go very far. One tug, and he easily pulls me back to the couch. Then he yanks, dragging me off balance.

I stagger and brace my hand against the back of the couch, but he doesn't relent until I collapse on top of him.

"Stay," he commands, patting my head like I'm a puppy. But his voice went deep again in that alarming, dizzying way that makes me question when I should be running away.

"Don't make me beg," he scolds when I hesitate. "It isn't sexy. You are, though. Even with that virginal act you have going on." He reaches out and tucks a piece of hair behind my ear, smoothing it into place. "How weird is that? You fuck a stranger more than once, and yet you still seem pure and shit. Perfect. You're perfect—"

"You're delirious," I stammer, but his suddenly loose tongue gives me an opportunity. "If you want me to stay, then tell me the truth. What did Hale see?"

"Can I get a raincheck on the third degree?" he asks softly.

If he's aiming to play on my pity, I think it's working. His filthy, sweat-soaked shirt feels hot against my cheek, but he doesn't smell as bad as he should. My nostrils flare as if to decipher why that might be. I've been with him long enough to know if he'd used cologne—he hasn't. But his scent doesn't exactly matter. Or so I tell myself.

"Then tell me something to make me stay," I counter. "In all honesty, I don't know anything about you."

"I wouldn't say that," he says in a teasing tone. "You know I have a son. A bossy as hell older sister. You even learned that my old man used to run the largest MC outfit in town. That has to account for something. And that my ex had a lot of fucking baggage, Silas being the least of it all."

"What happened back there wasn't just some stupid fight, was it?" I ask despite his plea.

"No." His fingers burrow into my hair, trapping me in an awkward position. Half kneeling on the floor, half pinned flat to his chest. "You look like the kind of girl who likes stories about fairy tale princesses and shit. Let me put it this way—Silas, that dark-haired bastard, fancies himself a king. He'll do anything for that crown. *He* is the villain of this story. Don't forget that for a fucking second."

"How?" I counter, my throat thickening. His voice is a dangerous weapon when it's raspy like that. Gravelly and throaty enough to resonate in my skin like thunder. It's enough to counteract the joking nature of his words, betraying the seriousness lurking underneath. "I want to know."

"How? By putting his nephew in danger," Daze growls. "By lying to my sister's face day in and out. By getting involved in shady fucking shit. The truth is, winning that fight is the start of my comeback and *his* downfall. I want to change, Frey, I do. But—I can't just fucking sit back and watch everything turn to shit under his command. I can't do that. I won't do that. There are much bigger things at stake now."

"Like what?" I question.

"That wig was so not your color, baby." He says, tugging on a piece of my natural hair. "You're a blondie, through and through."

"Answer the question." I form a fist and lightly punch his chest. "It has to be bad if you were going to jump off a bridge because of it."

"Jump..." His tongue flits along his lower lip as if he's tasting the word, marveling at how it sounds when said out loud. His eyes lower to mine, but they're darker than they should be. Sterner—as if for the first time, he's dropping the playful act. "I know you have the tortured rich girl thing going on, but do you have any idea who you are?" He swipes the swollen pad of his thumb across my upturned cheek and frowns. "Daughter of the holy politician. The man who makes it his fucking mission to 'eradicate evil from the city.'" He parrots Father's musical baritone. "Do you have any idea of what some people might do to gain control over a man like that?" He observes me and shakes his head. "No, I don't think you do."

He lets me go and shifts, forcing me to back away. Partially crouched on the floor, I watch him stand, surprisingly steady on his feet despite how he clutches his head with one hand.

"I'm gonna take a shower," he says, starting for the bathroom. His face is so swollen his lecherous smirk barely registers as he adds, "Care to join me?"

He expects me to say no, of course. I probably should, like good ol' Frey.

But he owes me. Not money per se, but something intangible that I can't describe. Something to erase the pain and the emptiness that threatens to sink in as he starts to close the door behind him. He owes it to me not to leave me alone.

A grunt escapes him as I brace my hand against the door before he can close it fully. The room is so small he has to press himself against the wall to allow me enough space to slip inside.

Aware of him watching, I strip my clothes before pulling back the flimsy curtain blocking the shower stall. He already has the water running, and I sigh as I climb in. "You coming?" I ask with my eyes closed as the water pelts me from above. It feels fucking amazing, and a part of me hopes he'll be the one to back down and run away.

Instead, he whistles low, and his footsteps resonate through the tile floor, lumbering in my direction.

"I should have known better," he mutters amid the hiss of swishing fabric. His shirt? A heavier thud makes me swallow hard. That didn't sound like cotton. Denim, maybe. I'm too chicken to open my eyes, rendering me blind as to how naked he is as his heat radiates against my back, driving me closer to the spigot. Warmer fingers part my hair, boldly stroking the strands all the way to my shoulders. "This girl was going to jump," he says thickly near my ear. "What's a little shower with a stranger to slow her down?"

"You could leave," I counter while tilting my head back to wet my hair.

"I could..."

A gasp rips from my throat as I feel him. He isn't wearing his jeans, but some sort of material brushes my hips rather than bare skin. His boxers? Not that it really matters. He towers above me from behind, and the sensation startles me into opening my eyes.

Of all the reckless things I've done...

This moment shouldn't feel so grounding. I shouldn't lean back, sensing firm muscle brace my weight with little effort. He feels good—I can't deny it. He feels real.

"But I don't plan on it, Frey," he reveals. "I'm not going anywhere. I'm right here."

A strangled sound catches in my throat, and I sense Daze stiffen.

The next second he spins me around as if knowing... My face

meets his chest, and I break. As my choked noises echo within the stall, I can't tell if I'm laughing or crying.

Maybe both.

He holds me anyway, wrapping me in massive arms that block the water from reaching me. "It's okay. I've got you," he mutters against my scalp, and I can feel the vibrations of his voice ripple down to my toes. "I've got you."

NINETEEN

WE TOWEL off what feels like an eternity later. As we leave the bathroom and enter his bedroom, he tosses me a pair of boxers and an oversized shirt while dressing himself in gray sweats. Then he climbs onto his bed as gingerly as an old man.

For whatever reason, I follow suit.

His hand brushes mine as I roll onto my side. His fingers curl, far too insistent to be by accident. Focusing on breathing, I shut my eyes, giving in to the exhaustion that takes over.

Then he lightly strokes my palm with his thumb. My pulse accelerates from his gentle gesture. My breathing hitches. All the erratic thoughts in my head seem to vanish.

Daze releases a small, sharp breath.

My eyes flutter open, and when I look at him, he's lying on

his side. His gaze is piercing, fixated on me, and it's evident that he doesn't intend to sleep just yet.

He slowly lifts his hand and caresses my face with the back of his fingers. A chill sweeps through me, and I'm drawn to him like a magnet. I involuntarily inch closer until our shoulders are touching, and his jaw clenches tight.

The waning daylight filters through the window, illuminating his beautifully-sculptured body covered in scars and ink. And *those striking, gray eyes.*

The way they look at me will be my downfall.

Yet, I find myself shifting closer. Closer. Even closer until his bare chest is flush with mine, but it's not enough. Before I can even make sense of it, I'm touching his face, brushing the loose strands of hair away from his eyes, giving me a better view.

"Good night," he says playfully, but I know he senses the same inexplicable emotion I do.

This moment feels different. Intimate.

Something I'm not quite used to.

He isn't either.

"I'm not used to being told to go to Hell and then chased after in one day," he says as his hand travels up my spine. He firmly grasps the back of my neck, and a soft breath escapes me.

"I'm not used to this," I say, using that word as a stand-in for many different things. I'm not used to intimacy. To violence. To the brutal clarity only he can give.

I should run from it. But I'm not.

"I owe you," he says as if I never spoke. "I don't like owing a debt, so I'll make you an offer. For you only—take what you want from me. Anything you want, it's yours…"

I can't tell if he's joking or not. Maybe it doesn't matter if he is. For this moment, I have him, and it's strangely *enough*. To the point that I feel tempted to commit yet another sin where he is concerned.

I want to be greedy.

"Tell me about how you 'almost' went to prison. Why did you say my father had something to do with it?"

He sighs. "You remember how I said Hale asked me to do something for him?"

I nod, feeling my stomach tighten. "What?"

"He wanted me to look into your church. Salvation or whatever—"

"Salvation is the outreach program," I say absently. "Covenant is our church. It's my father's take on the Protestant faith and its core tenants, but with an emphasis on charity and virtue."

My throat dries as I realize how little of those ideals I've lived up to lately.

"Salvation is my father's pet project. He's helped many people through it."

"Oh, I'm sure he has," Daze says. "Hale thought it was a front for something. I'm not sure what. When I started digging, let's just say someone turned up dead, and I got thrown in lockup and threatened with a murder charge."

I just stare at him. He sounds different when he's being truthful. Less playful and more... Cold. He doesn't have the energy left to put up a front anymore.

When he doesn't elaborate, all I can ask is, "Did you do it?"

He meets my gaze and holds it. "No. And the cops had nothing on me, either. That's the strange part. The law is that after forty-eight hours they have to let you go. Somehow, due to a 'paperwork' mix-up, I was in there for three months. By the time I got out, Hale was dead, and the truth is, I don't know exactly why."

"But you think my father has something to do with it?"

He flicks his gaze up to the ceiling. "Let's just say I had a hunch. The same hunch I had to keep an eye on you with your brother gone. That intuition hasn't failed me yet."

I swallow hard, overwhelmed by the genuine concern I hear in his voice. "You really care that much? About someone you didn't even know?"

He does his best to shrug and winds up grimacing. "Sometimes you just get a sense for who someone is. They have a look about them. A feeling."

My heartbeat begins to race. "Are you saying that you know me?"

His sly smile returns. "I'm saying I haven't regretted dragging some crazy Blondie from the edge of a bridge. Not yet, anyway."

And the strange part is that I haven't regretted letting him.

Breathing him in, I close the space between us and press my mouth against his. Without thinking through the consequences, I slip my tongue through the seam of his lips. He grunts in alarm, letting his hands graze over every curve of my body. An ache settles between my legs, and my inner thighs become slick with arousal. Seeking relief, I push my lower half against him out of pure desperation, needing more.

When he winces, I have the sense of mind to realize that it isn't out of pleasure. He's still in pain, and I pull back, watching him force a smirk while his eyes glisten with discomfort.

"You think I could get a raincheck?" he asks.

But then I remember...

There is more to sinning than just fornication. He taught me that, after all. Without revealing my intentions, I settle on my knees beside him, placing my hand on his chest. Gingerly, I ease him onto his back and reach for the waistband of his pants.

Confusion displaces his grimace, and he tries to sit up. "Wait."

"It's okay," I say. How I manage to speak at all? I'll never know. His movements only serve to wrench his pants partway down, revealing what lurks underneath.

The married women in Covenant—when they dared to speak amongst themselves in hushed whispers—spoke about what happened between a man and a woman. The female had a holy place in which a man would place his manhood for the sole purpose of making a baby.

They glossed over its description in vague whispers. None of them ever mentioned how beautiful a man can seem. Their pious term doesn't seem right, and I decide to use a different term. *His* term.

Daze's cock springs free, twitching against his abdomen, and I'm struck dumb by the sight.

The expression on my face must erase his concerns because he lifts his arms, his biceps flexing, and rests them beside his head on the pillow.

I hesitate, unsure of what to do next.

"Your mouth," he suggests in a whisper. "You can use your mouth."

A flashback of him going down on me in the bathroom plays back in my mind, yet I have no personal experience with this.

"I've never..." I hesitate, unsure.

"It's okay." He grins, and there's a faint sparkle in his eye. "You don't have to—"

Trusting him blindly, I lean downward, grasping him with my hand, sneaking a peek at his face just in time to witness his mouth fall open as I press my lips to his tip. Encouraged, I part my lips and brush him tentatively with my tongue, praying I'm doing this right.

And his moans prove I am.

"Fuck, baby," he groans with satisfaction as I slowly bob my head, still holding him steady with one hand.

Taking him out of my mouth for a moment, I look into his eyes. "Like this?" I whisper, circling my lips around him, gliding my tongue down his length.

"Yes," he rushes out in one quick breath. "Oh, fuck." He doesn't act how I did when slung over the sink. His reaction is fearless. Primal. Teeth bared, he thrusts his hips from the bed and runs his hands through my damp hair. "Just. Like. That."

I moan in relief, relishing his taste, pleased that I'm doing it right. My entire body hums triumphantly, inspiring new reactions I can't ignore. My nipples turn into hard, red buds as I suck him harder, and he guides my hand lower so I'm cupping the flesh below his shaft.

"You sure you haven't done this before?" Despite the taunt, his breathing becomes shallow. His eyes are narrowed to slits, eyelids fluttering, as he runs his hands through my hair. "You're doing such a good job, baby, but I want to be inside you. *Really* inside you." He fumbles for his nightstand and fishes a condom from a drawer. He rips open the packet with his teeth before handing it to me.

After watching me struggle to slip it on, he takes my hand and shows me how. It's an education I savor, knowing it will come in handy next time.

Because there *will* be a next time.

For now, he yanks my shirt over my head while I do the same with my shorts.

"Come here, Frey," he orders softly, pulling me onto him.

Naked, I straddle his waist, reaching behind to position him at my entrance. He arches into me easily as my body molds to him. I press my palms on his chest, feeling the warmth that radiates from him.

"You're such a good girl, Frey," he says, taking my breasts in his hands. "You know that?"

A quiet breath escapes me as I rise slowly before lowering myself back onto him, creating the perfect rhythm. He traces his thumbs over my nipples, and the sensation feels electrifying.

My eager cries fill the room as I rock my hips. He feels so deep, beyond buried to the hilt. Heightening the sensation, he firmly grasps my hips, digging his fingertips into my skin. There's the sound of skin smacking as I rock into him, setting my own pace and taking every ounce of control.

Power.

It feels incredible.

"Daze," I call out breathlessly, grinding myself against his pelvis. The friction builds and builds before pushing me far over the edge.

Crying out to him, my body convulses. I see stars behind my eyelids.

"Frey, baby," he grunts, bucking his hips while caressing what feels like every part of my body. "You're so fucking beautiful. Like an angel." He reaches for my collarbone and curves his fingers around my cross. Pulling tight on the chain, he thrusts into me deeper and finds his release. "Damn, you're a fucking angel, sent just for me."

Collapsing beside him seconds later, he drags me into his arms... and simply *holds* me.

And for a second—just one—I consider the dangerous possibility that a person could be more dizzying than the wildest high.

And worthy of the most grievous sin.

Starved, I enter the kitchen and make myself a sandwich. He joins me not long after, with a cigarette in hand, and fishes his own snack from the fridge. Then we eat in silence, watching each other from opposite ends of the room.

Finally, he draws his half-eaten sandwich away and asks with his mouth partially full, "Ain't this a sin?"

"What?" I feel my brows furrow. I'm seated on the couch, and from the corner of my eye, I swear I can make out his bloodstains on the material.

"Your father is some hotshot preacher man, isn't he? Shouldn't you be in church or some shit?"

"And shouldn't you be at a gang meeting?" I spit back, but there's no real malice in my voice. He has a point. "Father's the Shepherd," I add, drawing my knees up beneath my chin. "Of the Covenant. They believe in Christianity but don't practice out of a typical church. They hold congregation wherever they feel the giving spirit." I finger a suspiciously dark splotch on a nearby cushion. It's definitely blood. "I could be praying right now for all you know."

"And your father just lets you wander around without a bodyguard? Even while he's running for fucking governor?"

I shrug. "He's busy." At least leading Covenant gives him a sanctimonious excuse for neglecting his children. "You want to know something really funny?" I tilt my head to observe his wary frown. "According to him, we can't even have a 'true' conversation until I repent and join his congregation. Though what he really wants is another trophy. Hale played the part for a while, the dutiful son."

He'd been a stranger then. Someone who looked at me and no longer saw his kid sister. Just a selfish, ugly burden.

"How did he get into drugs?" Daze asks. "Don't give me that look," he adds in response to my raised eyebrow. "I do listen when you talk."

"I'm not sure exactly when it happened," I admit, crossing my arms over my chest. "But he changed. He got angrier. Meaner. Paranoid. It was like he knew something but wouldn't talk to me about what." I may not be able to remember him clearly, but I remember watching him pace throughout the house, always distracted. "He stopped going to congregation meetings. Then he..."

"Why do you blame your dad?" Daze wonders in between ravenous bites of his sandwich. "Lack of parental guidance?"

"No." I look down at my hands, watching how they tremble, still holding slivers of meat and bread. "When Hale died, I searched his room. I found bank statements listing transfers from my dad's account into Hale's. A lot of money. And Father isn't stupid. He had to have known something wasn't..." I shake my head as my eyes burn. "You don't give someone with a problem that kind of money."

"Have you talked to him about it?"

"I can't." I tug at my cross and sigh. "As long as I'm a 'sinner,' I don't matter to him. I'm just a statistic to help or hinder his campaign."

"The savior of the city," Daze says, once again channeling Father's bravado. "What do you know about his little volunteer program?"

"Salvation?" I bite my lower lip. The words could be a mocking quip, but he's using that serious tone again. "Hale called it a scam. I know my father is staking his election campaign on the fact that he eradicated forty percent of overall crime. Like your little gang, for instance."

He chuckles and draws back, leaning against the counter. Even wearing a ratty pair of sweats and bruised to hell and back, he cuts an imposing silhouette. His good eye observes me intently, missing nothing from my nervous swallow down to the way my gaze dances across the muscles flexing beneath his skin. "You want to know more about my gang, Blondie?" The corner of his mouth quirks—as much of a smirk as he can attempt. "No. I don't think you can handle it. They aren't all bad, though. Once upon a time, we had real structure. Maybe even respect."

"I'm guessing before you were in charge?" I wonder innocently.

His mouth returns to that hard, unusually serious line, and I squirm, uneasy.

"Let's say it's just like your father's little cult—only we worship a different kind of God."

"Money?" I say, hazarding a guess. "Are you some kind of dealer, Daze?"

"No." He cuts his gaze away from me, his jaw tight. "Not anymore. But when I was in the Saints, we took our code seriously. Maybe that doesn't mean anything to you, coming from a former 'dealer,' but we lived by it. Some of us were willing to die by it..."

Something in his tone makes me swallow hard and that itching, tightening feeling in my chest returns. It's time for a change of subject, but when one comes to mind, it's more dangerous than heroin. "Where's Sammy's mom?"

He looks up sharply, and his body stiffens, poised on the tips of his toes. He eyes me for so damn long. It feels like I've been invisible my entire life before him. With one glance, he sees too much. All of me. "Dead."

I could ask him how, parroting the words I heard Silas say. But I don't. I eye Daze instead. God, he shouldn't be attractive in this moment. Maybe he's not—not exactly. His body is a distraction my mind seems keen to utilize. I can't help picturing him injury-free, a member of a gang Father made sound synonymous with the devil himself.

"See something you like?"

I flinch and meet his gaze again. "Thank you."

I don't say for what. He nods anyway like he understands what I can't put into words. *Thank you for ruining my pity party. Thank you for stopping me. Thank you.*

"You might want to hold off on the gratefulness, though," he adds. "Give me time to sleep off this headache. One more night. Tomorrow, I'll tell you the truth I've been dancing around, though you aren't stupid. I'm sure you've come to a few conclusions of your own."

Conclusions involving Hale's suspicion of our father, perhaps. Or why one of Father's men was at the fight ring? Or...

"Tomorrow," Daze scolds, nudging my chin with his thumb. "For now, let's sleep."

I try not to think about everything I'm ignoring by staying with him. Father's dinner with Colton, among them.

It's easier than it should be to push them to the back of my mind and focus only on Daze.

We make our way back to the bedroom and lie beneath the sheets, bodies intertwined.

"Before the fight... in the locker room... you mentioned how a man's old lady would give him a kiss for good luck—" I begin. "And I kissed you."

His face softens, and there's a flash of vulnerability behind his gaze. I've never seen him look quite this sincere.

"Does that mean I'm yours, Daze?" I ask, staring endlessly into his eyes.

"What? My old lady?" He brings me closer, crushing me against the warm, solid frame of his chest. "Do you want to be?" he asks, his tone suddenly quiet. Overly cautious.

Do I? My pulse quickens with each slow breath. And within seconds, I find myself nodding, unable to put my feelings into words.

After Hale's death, I've been spiraling, feeling lost and unsure of myself. With Daze, I feel wanted for the first time in...too long to remember. I feel safe.

Alive.

"I need to hear you," he grits out, tracing the contour of my face with his thumb. "Open that pretty little mouth for me, Frey, and use your words."

"Yes," I whisper.

"Since the first moment I saw you standing on the edge of the bridge—" he slowly lets out, studying my face, "—you were mine then. And you're mine, now."

And he holds me close as we drift off to sleep.

TWENTY

I WAKE UP SIGHING, languidly stretching out my limbs.
For a second, I feel a tendril of lingering guilt—how can I feel
so relaxed at a time like this, with the truth of Hale's death
still shrouded in mist? Then a nagging pleasure drowns out
any doubt. I earned this peace, if only for a few seconds.

I deserve it. So, I burrow into Daze's side guilt free and relish
his heat on my skin and his low, sleepy growl of approval. I let
my mind skip ahead, imagining all the many ways he can help
me forget my worries for the rest of the day.

But then the world explodes. A thud resonates from the
other room, and Daze lurches upright just as the door flies
open, slamming against the wall. A figure stands at the other
end, but they aren't his sister Lyra. A man looms there,
dressed in dark colors, his arm extended before him.

"Don't fucking move," he snarls, training an object over
Daze's chest. Black. Rectangular. My mind registers it belat-

edly as the man steps forward, revealing another figure behind him.

Instantly, I recognize his eyes—and the cold, piercing quality to them. Silas.

"Did you really think I wouldn't recognize her?" He steps forward and inclines his head in my direction while the man with the gun inches toward me, still focused on Daze.

"What the fuck is this?" Daze's tone is carefully controlled. He reaches for my wrist and wrenches me behind him. Then he grabs a sheet and drapes it over me, ignoring how the man with the weapon tenses at the action. "You know the rules. You stay in your territory, and you stay *out* of mine—"

"You want to talk about rules now? It's a good thing I knew better than to trust your lying ass," Silas says, his lips quirked. "You stick your nose up at getting your hands dirty, but here you are, trying to undercut me after walking away with your moral tail between your legs. So tell me—have you already sent a ransom letter off to her father? How much did you think you could get for her? A few grand? A mil? I'm sure that's the only reason you intervened, but I guess you didn't get the memo. She belongs to someone else. He won't give you a fucking dime."

Confusion alone spurs me to croak out a question from over Daze's shoulder. "What are you talking about?"

"Don't fucking move," the man with the gun snarls.

Silas chuckles. "You always did have a thing for damsels, Day.

I wonder who tipped you off. Chris? Ben? Either way, they'll pay—"

"No one had to tell me shit," Daze growls. "I know you, Silas. I know the shit you're into. It was only a matter of time before you got in over your head. You think your mysterious benefactor is some big fucking secret? Bullshit. We all know that the Saints don't have your loyalty. I know who your true master is."

"Is that so? Well, I know that following you almost led the outfit to the brink of ruin. But you were too damn busy fucking around with booze and women to give a damn. At least under me, the Saints will be respected again. It's only a matter of time before our legacy extends beyond a few crumbling dens and cage fights. We will own this city." He turns to his henchman and nods toward me. "Get some clothes on her and get her in the truck. Hurry the fuck up—"

The man doesn't get the chance to move before Daze practically shoves me into the closet and positions himself in front of me. And as if it's a sign from above, I notice the Saints jacket buried in the far back, out of reach. "You goddamn prick," Daze snarls. "You want her? You go through me. This time, don't hide behind a patsy to take the fall. You fucking face *me*."

"You don't call the shots anymore," Silas says harshly. "But if you want to play, who am I to stop you?"

With Daze in my way, I can't see a thing—I can only hear. A sickening thud. A groan. Suddenly, Daze sinks to his knees, and Silas pushes past him. In his hand is another gun he doesn't hesitate to point my way.

I go numb. For a second, anything he says goes in one ear and out the other. He has to shout before I finally comprehend. "I told you to get dressed."

My limbs jerk into action, and I crouch for the clothing still piled on the floor. I risk glancing over at Daze, and my heart stops. He's hunched on his side, clutching his head. Did Silas hit him?

"Hurry up!"

Silas waves his hand closer to my face, reinforcing the threat. Looking up, I can't take my eyes off the weapon, but somehow, I manage to shimmy into Daze's shorts under the probing eyes of the two men. The second I'm decent, Silas lunges for my wrist and drags me away from the bed. I claw at his hand, nails drawn, and he yanks, knocking me to my knees.

"Your father doesn't want you harmed, little girl," he tells me. "But if you don't want to play nice, I may have to make an exception."

He could have struck me, and I doubt the blow would disorient me as much as that one word does. Father?

"You're dead," Daze rasps, trying and failing to stand. His old wound has reopened, and fresh blood paints his face in garish hues of scarlet.

"Your threats don't hold any more sway," Silas says, chuckling. He tugs me to my feet and cinches my neck from behind. Using the grip as a leash, he forces me into the living room with a debilitating shove.

Voice thick with agony, Daze calls out. "You do this, and it's war, Silas. Fucking war."

My spine tenses. I recognize that icy voice of his. A dangerous warning is concealed in the threat, one that Silas doesn't seem to take seriously.

He laughs, shoving me toward the door. Contorting my neck, I strain for one last glimpse of Daze—and it's as if my gaze alone spurs him into action. He leaps from the bedroom like a caged animal who just broke free, and his fist collides with Silas' face in one crippling blow.

Like that night in the ring, he seems electrified by primal instinct. Unstoppable.

Until Silas' pistol comes down hard on Daze's head, and he goes limp immediately, crashing against the kitchen counters.

"No!" Any move I make is quickly restricted as Silas cinches my arm and muscles me back.

"Now, don't do anything stupid, Frances," he snarls into my ear. "Or I'll tell Frank here to shoot this motherfucker, and trust me, he won't miss."

"We got to move, boss," Frank orders, gesturing to the front door with the gun.

I obey, feeling pitiful. Defenseless.

Terrified.

It's an overwhelming, helpless dread more powerful than even what I felt at the bridge. A part of me wants to give in now. Let him shoot me. I can't experience that pain again.

But Daze is the last thing I see before I'm dragged into the hall entirely. It shouldn't be possible, but concern for him drives out the fear, if only for a second.

I can't give in now. Not if he's okay. Not if Hale's killer is still out there. Not if my father being entwined with Silas more than once isn't a coincidence.

So, I bite my tongue and try to channel everything Daze taught me that day in the gym.

I fight. No matter how loud I scream, kick, and flail my arms, I don't get close to breaking free. I just tire myself out, panting with the effort it takes to struggle.

But I don't feel the fear anymore. Not even as they haul me out of the building and into a dark, enclosed space. Fighting to regain control of my breathing, I strain my eyes to make out anything of use. Any potential exit.

A sudden rush of air has me turning toward it—and I don't even see the blow coming.

Smack.

A sharp pain shoots through my head, and everything goes black.

TWENTY-ONE

DAZE

MY HEAD IS POUNDING like a motherfucker. *Shit.* No high leaves a hangover this damn rough. I try to remember...

And she's the first thing to come to mind. *Frey.*

Pushing myself up from the floor, I scan the room in search of her as it all comes rushing back.

Silas. That stupid, twisted son of a bitch. He went too far this time. He crossed a line.

And there's nothing I can fucking do...

They wouldn't have taken her to the usual compound. No. They'd bring her somewhere more secure. But where?

"Fuck," I bark, staggering to the living room, searching erratically for my phone.

Fuck, fuck, fuck.

I nearly tear the whole place apart until I find it buried between the couch cushions. Then, I dial a number from memory, fighting back lingering unease. I can get on a moral high horse later. Desperate times and shit.

Ben can't get involved, given his proximity to the crew. Neither can Chris. As I go down the list of potential allies, it's pretty fucking short.

Unless...

I only know of one sick bastard twisted enough to outsmart the Saints. One psychopath capable of going against Silas.

As if drawn to the danger, he answers on the first ring.

"I only gave one man this number. You better be him." His voice is as unhinged as I remember. Like he's always on the verge of a murderous tirade.

It's music to my damn ears.

"Daze?"

"It's me, Damien. I need that favor you owe me," I tell him.

A sane man might ask questions. Not him. He doesn't even hesitate, "When and where?"

I sigh. Relieved? I don't know. All I can think of is her. That innocent fucking face and those wide, green eyes. "Now," I say. "We'll need extra muscle. How fast can you get here?"

"We're already on our way, D," Damien grunts. "Just remember, nice and clean isn't my style."

"Good," I snap. Silas has it coming. If he wants to go to war, then so be it. "Bring me all you got."

With that, the line goes dead, and there isn't time to second-guess the choice I've just made.

By going after Silas directly, I'm signing myself up for a lifetime of hell. He and his crew will never let me live this down. In that case...

Why not call in the devil?

~ Daze and Frey's story continues in Rogue Angel ~

ABOUT LANA SKY

Lana Sky is a reclusive writer in the United States who spends most of her time daydreaming about complex male characters and parenting her Cockapoo Joey. She writes dark, twisted romance across several genres. Her titles include everything from mafia romance to vampires.

facebook.com/AuthorLanaSky

x.com/lanasky101

amazon.com/author/lanasky

pinterest.com/lanasky101

goodreads.com/lanasky

instagram.com/lanasky101

bookbub.com/authors/lana-sky

tiktok.com/@author_lana_sky